TWELVE DATES OF CHRISTMAS

ALSO BY M.T. KNIGHTS

Re-Gifting Christmas, Holly Springs Romance Book 3

TWELVE DATES OF CHRISTMAS

HOLLY SPRINGS ROMANCE, BOOK 2

M.T. KNIGHTS

This is a work of fiction. Names, characters, places, and incidents either are the product of the author's imagination or are used fictitiously. Any resemblance to actual persons, living or dead, events, or locales is entirely coincidental.

Copyright © 2019 by M.T. Knights
Cover design by Blue Water Books

First print edition: September 2019
All rights reserved. No part of this book may be reproduced or used in any manner without written permission of the copyright owner except for the use of quotations for the purpose of a book review.

1

IVY

I opened my eyes and yawned, like one of those Disney princesses after a restful night. I hadn't had a restful night of sleep in months. The very idea that I was rested shot me upright in bed. I shouldn't be rested. I also shouldn't be waking to sunlight in a quiet room.

It was a school day, after all, and my week with the kids. After Derick left, they were my sole responsibility on school days. I looked at my alarm clock. It was already after seven. I pushed the buttons to see why my alarm hadn't gone off, but there wasn't even one scheduled.

I grabbed my phone, my second alarm, but looking through it, I was surprised to see that again, nothing had been set. It was ridiculous. I always woke at 5:00 a.m. to my alarms, regardless of how late I'd been up working on my business plans or helping the kids with homework the night before. It didn't make sense. As I frantically looked through my phone to ensure that all the rest of my alarms were still in place, my phone buzzed and rang.

I relinquished a knowing smile. It was Angie Segmeeler, my longest and closest friend.

"Hey!" I said, my voice still a bit groggy. I expected her to ask about our plans for the weekend or ask if I had time to do lunch that afternoon. But when her voice came on the line, her words were far from the casual 'Hey, let's do lunch,' I'd been expecting.

"Oh good, you answered. I've been at the Mayor's office all morning." Her voice was higher than normal, and the cadence was off. Angie was the Mayor's assistant, a job that she claimed to love but mostly complained about. Her rapid speech suggested this was more than just a simple complaint phone call though.

I looked at the clock on the side of my bed again.

"All morning? It's barely past seven…" All morning was a bit dramatic. My mornings typically started early, but Angie was single and as a government worker, she wasn't needed into work until nine. I was pretty certain that most mornings, she'd barely rolled out of bed by seven.

"I know! I've been here since five trying to fix the mess I woke up to. I have to fix it all before the parade and tree lighting tonight. It's a complete disaster. I should have gone with *you* from the beginning. I'm still sorry about that. Had the mayor not insisted we pick another party planning company—ugh." She groaned. "I don't even know what to do at this point."

I didn't bother to address the issue again. Of course it had hurt me at the time, but it wasn't worth saying anything now.

"All the plans and preparations for the town's Christmas celebrations are out the window. Gone, Ivy. All of them!"

"The designer didn't share the plans with you?" I said, more in disbelief than to argue.

"She called last night. Last night! On my personal number and I didn't answer because I was on a date with Mr. Handsome. Of course I wasn't going to answer. I think the party planner knew to call then. The nerve! She left a message to inform me that she could no longer continue working on the Christmas project. The Christmas project that begins tonight! I just can't even. A message. Like we're some sleazy couple who hooked up a week ago, and now she's become disinterested. We've been planning this event for a year! A YEAR! What kind of company or person cancels a year-in-the-making event on the day of?"

"Ange." I spoke calmly, trying to get her to stop her diatribe.

"An entire year of working together and they break up with the mayor's office in a message! As if bankruptcy just comes out of nowhere." She went on, completely ignoring me.

"Angie…" Again, my voice was a steady beat to counteract her hysteria.

"If I ever see her, or anyone from that company again, I will find so much joy in wrapping my hands around their slimy little necks and squeezing until their beady little eyes start to bulge and then I'll—"

"Angela!" I yelled before she revealed her entire murder plot. I spared a glance at the clock. Shoot, it was already seven fifteen. I needed to be getting the kids up right now.

With the phone in one hand, I sat up and yanked my down comforter from my otherwise content body; the sudden cool air hitting my bare legs caused goosebumps to appear.

"Sorry," Angela groaned. "I just don't know what to do."

"I know." I sighed, trying to rub warmth into my legs.

"You said they'd been planning for over a year, though. The design company had to have left those plans with someone in the Mayor's office." I forced myself to stand and walk to the master bathroom. I pulled out my toothbrush and did my best to quietly clean the nasty morning breath from my mouth as Angie went on.

"They were so adamant about their work and had all the resources to prove that they had it under control, I didn't bother for many updates. I'm going to get fired. I'll lose my house and end up living on the street, bumming change off of people outside The Pub. I just know it!" Angie's voice rose an octave and I could tell she was about to spiral out of control again.

Another glance at the clock told me I did not have time to shower like I normally would or really finish this conversation. I settled for a splash of water on my face and a ponytail as I did my best to calm my best friend.

"Ange, you called the best party planner in town. I think we can figure this out. You have the tree already; the town provides most of the ornaments. The parade is basically organized by the high school and the businesses. Relax. We can do this and it will be amazing."

Scanning my closet, I sighed when my eyes landed on the full basket of dirty clothes. Like a grungy college student, I pulled the jeans from the floor and fanned them out before squeezing into them, nearly dropping the phone as I wedged it between my shoulder and ear.

"Oh, the parade! There's no town float. The Christmas parade cannot happen without the town float. I don't even think we have a Santa Claus." Angie sighed.

"I'm sure we can find one. And I can help you put a float together. We have all day," I said, hiding my own panic over the late start to my day. "The parade isn't until six tonight. We've got this."

I knew my day was already busy, but I could help my best friend get the parade and stuff together and then she could figure out the rest of the town's Christmas plans later.

"How are we going to light the tree?" Angie asked, as if just realizing it needed to be done.

"Oh, uh..." I pulled the sweatshirt that I'd hung on my bedpost last night over my head, the phone squished against my cheek, muffling my voice. "I'm sure we can get help with that." I wasn't sure where, but didn't have a better response as I bounded out my bedroom door and down the hall to get the kids out of bed. Hopefully they'd laid their clothes out for today last night, like I'd asked.

"Okay, okay. If we can get through tonight, we can tackle the Christmas Gala tomorrow." Angie said, her voice calming a bit.

The *Christmas Gala?* I didn't dare express my alarm, not when she had just calmed down. We would handle one thing at a time.

"You wanna meet at The Bell to hash tonight out? I'll buy breakfast," she added in a pleading sing-song voice.

"Sure. Let me get the kids ready and off to school. I can meet you in thirty minutes or so."

"Thank you so much, Ivy! I don't know what I would do without you."

I swung open the girl's bedroom door. Both beds were empty.

"I mean really," Angie went on. "We should have gone with you in the first place. I knew I should have, I just..."

"Stop. I know. We've been over it, and I'm over it." I took the few steps to Harrison's room only to see his light on, his bed also empty. They must have gotten up before me and snuck downstairs to watch television.

"Look, I gotta go. Don't apologize; things are good. Let's just focus on what we can do today." I took a deep breath and turned to the stairs, hoping the kids had the intuition to at least get dressed before turning on the television they weren't supposed to watch before breakfast.

"Thanks, Ives. You're the best friend I could ever ask for."

"Since third grade," I responded.

"Since third grade." I can hear the smile in her tone. "See you in a bit."

I disconnected the call before I spotted the three little heads illuminated by the glow of the television in an otherwise dark living room. I cringed as I saw what they were watching and eating.

Mallory, perched on the giant bean bag with her hand in a bag of chips, crunched away happily while Jenny and Harrison lazily wrestled for control of the store-bought cookie dough as their eyes glazed over a cartoon that's usually not allowed in the house.

The situation called for some intervention and some serious mothering, but I partially blamed myself for not getting up and going before they did. A good mother would have woken hours before her children, made them a balanced breakfast and ensured they had not turned the television on until they'd made their beds, showered and dressed for the day. She would also make sure her children never missed the bus.

I glanced at the clock on the microwave. Fifteen minutes until the bus showed up. The only mothering that time allowed for was to take the junk food from their hands with a disapproving look and urge them up the stairs to get dressed, without a shower or their beds made.

With cookie dough and chips in each hand, I yelled demands and threatened punishments, silently cursing myself for blaming them when I was the one who had screwed up.

"I can't believe you guys. Why didn't you wake me? It's

after seven." I glanced at the clock. "Oh crap, it's seven forty. None of you are even dressed for school. Mal, go change. Fast! And then help Harrison. I'll take Jenny."

The three of them sat there and stared at me like I was speaking some foreign language, their mouths open as the glare from the television glowed all around them, making them look like tiny little confused angels who I'd just yelled at for being kids.

There just wasn't time. I reached down and took a hold of Jenny's chubby, little, cookie dough covered hand and urged her up the stairs, calling from behind me, "Move it, guys! Bus gets here in ten minutes."

Dressing a sticky four-year-old who wants no part in getting dressed is like trying to put clothes on a wild monkey who'd just bathed in a vat of honey. It's not something I'd do well on a day when I wasn't in a hurry, but today? Let's just say the fact that she had a shirt and pants on was enough for me not to notice the giant clump of cookie dough in my hair or her mismatched socks. I slicked her hair down with water and urged her to find her shoes. She was four, perfectly capable of putting her own shoes on while I checked on Harrison. Or so I thought.

I peeked my head into his room and was beyond grateful that I had been blessed with a daughter like Mal. Harrison was dressed, with hair done and shoes on. Mal sat on the floor tying his sneakers. It was not the first time I'd thought about how much better she was at being an adult than I was. She'd managed to get two kids dressed and ready in the time it took me to scrape cookie dough out of my hair and put a toddler's pants on backward.

"Thanks, Mal," I called before ducking out of her room to coax Jenny down the stairs to eat some kind of nutrients. I plopped her on the kitchen counter and handed her a banana and forced a smile.

"Yuck!" She threw her little fist on top of the banana and the peel oozed white mush out its sides.

I inhaled and closed my eyes. Knowing I couldn't trust my words, I scooped the remnants of the banana off the table and tossed it in the trash just before Mallory and Harrison hopped up to the counter.

"Are we going ice skating tonight still?" Harrison asked with bright innocent six-year-old eyes. He fiddled with the zipper on his jacket.

I had totally forgotten. With my updated busy schedule after Angie's panicked phone call, we wouldn't have time to go ice skating. But I didn't have the heart to break that sweet smile. Instead, I just returned it with one of my own and did my best to prepare him for the letdown I'd hopefully have the confidence to deliver later.

"If we can get everything done that we need to before it gets too late," I said. I didn't bother to explain that the things I needed to get done would never, in a million years, be done by seven tonight.

"I don't think I'll have too much homework, Mom. My report is due today and Mrs. Hunter doesn't usually assign a bunch of stuff right after a big homework assignment," Mallory said encouragingly.

"Oh that's right, your report is today! Are you ready?"

"Yep. I've got my poster by the door and my paper in my bag. It'll be a breeze. Mars is such an easy topic, and since I'm the only one who picked it, I'm basically going to get an A."

"Good job, hon! I wish I could see you present it."

"Uh, you can. Remember? She invited parents. I thought you were coming."

The bus's breaks squeaked outside the kitchen window. Of course. Not enough time to let her down easy either.

"Right. What I meant to say was I am so excited to come today."

Just another thing to add to my list of the impossible.

Mal's nine-year-old smile returned as she reached for an apple out of the fruit bowl. I handed Harrison one as well, but he shook his head.

"Banana?" I asked.

"You know I don't like plain fruit, Mom." He said the word 'mom' like I'd just committed the most embarrassing blunder of all time.

"Right."

"Adrianne's mom lets her drink protein shakes for breakfast. Why can't I do that? Or even a smoothie!"

"I don't have time to make a smoothie." I leave out the part that I think Adrianne's mom is insane for letting her daughter drink a protein shake for breakfast. It's not like she's an adult on some diet. It wouldn't be nice to talk bad about my son's friend's mom in front of him, even though I secretly despise that Adrianne and the silly ideas she puts into Harrison's head.

"Maybe if you got up earlier…" Harrison interrupted my judgement of others and brought it right back to me. He was right.

Mal shoved Harrison in the side and shook her head.

The bus's horn honked and what little time I had to instill love, hope and nutrients into my two oldest was gone. Instead of more nagging, I bent down and opened my arms for hugs.

"I love you guys!"

"Love you too, Mom," Harrison and Mal said in unison before sprinting out the door toward the awaiting yellow bus, leaving with promises of fun I wouldn't be able to provide and an imbalanced breakfast.

I looked to Jenny. She'd gotten a hold of my phone and was playing some alphabet game. At least she was learning, I told myself.

"You ready, princess?" I asked.

"What about breakfast?"

"We'll grab something on the way. You don't have to be there until nine thirty," I said as I helped her into her coat and grabbed the little backpack that she'd filled with princess crowns, bouncy balls and rocks.

It wasn't until we were in the car and almost to The Bell that I glanced into the backseat and see only a pair of wet, mismatched socks covering her shoeless feet.

2

DERICK

*T*he County building was pretty dead. Which wasn't surprising in a town with a population of two thousand. But I had sort of hoped for a line to wait in to build my courage. This was a big step. I'd been doing carpentry jobs here and there for years, but it had never occurred to me to make it a profession until I had to. Over the last four months or so, as I'd put an effort into my work, I'd really seen it take off. I was even starting to get phone calls from people out of town who wanted to hire me.

It made sense to make the whole thing official, and it felt like the right time.

I stepped up to the counter where Rebecca Wagstaff sat twirling a pen in her hand as she stared at her Sudoku book, clicking her tongue. Becca had been in elementary school with me; she was always smart, but somewhat of an oddball. Not in a bad way, she just liked to say things that were, well, a little off.

I cleared my throat.

"Hold yer ponies, dancing queen, this ain't the DMV here. I'll help ya when I'm ready."

Stuff like that. I nodded and put my forms on the counter to wait for her to be ready.

"And there it is, my friends! The three goes in the middle!" She laughed and then slammed her book on the counter beside my paperwork.

"Now, what can I do ya for? Oh whoa, hold up! I know this guy. How the heck are ya, Derick?"

"I'm doing well, Becca. How are you?"

"Well besides kicking Sudoku trash, I'd say I'm just all right. You know, livin' the dream. Working at the ol' County Building is just a step shy of driving taxi, so I'd say I'm pulling out okay."

"Definitely," I said, hoping my response was somewhat accurate to the nonsense she'd just spilled out.

"Right. Well, what can I do ya for?"

"I just came in to get these papers filed so I can get my business license and secure that warehouse on lot forty-eight."

"Oooh, lot forty-eight is finally getting some attention. Good pick. I've been eyeing her for years."

"Uh, thanks." I mostly picked it because it was the closest open building that could store my equipment and lumber.

"Great, well." Becca looked over the paperwork and stamped a few things before getting to the last page and smiling. "It looks like ya got all your ducks in a line. I'll just need to see that two-hundred dollar processing fee and you'll be the official owner of…what was it you were gonna call your warehouse?"

"It's not a warehouse. It's a…oh, never mind. Winston's Custom Designs."

"Oh, like your last name. That makes sense."

"Yeah."

Becca held out her hand.

"Right." I fished into my back pocket and pulled out my wallet. I swallowed hard as I placed the card in her hand and said a quick prayer that this really was what I was supposed to do with my life.

After a quick scan of the card, another couple of signatures and a few more awkward moments with Becca, I was leaving the County building and heading to my truck.

I pushed through the oversized exit doors and into the parking lot. Next to what I assumed were a handful of nice, government-issue sedans sat my beaten down truck. With stack of papers in hand, I walked to the passenger side door and reached my hand in through the open window to unlock and open the door.

I slid the stack of signed and certified papers inside the glove box for safekeeping before I crawled over the seat and middle console to reach the driver's side. The car may have been old and slightly challenging to get into, but it always started after a few tries and it had served me well since the day I bought it off my brother nearly twenty years ago.

After the morning's events, I was the proud owner of warehouse forty-eight, soon to be my new cabinetry workshop and thus all my hopes and dreams. I had taken the first step to my financial freedom and success and that called for a little celebration.

I deserved a nice breakfast, one I didn't have to make it. The Bell was only a fifteen-minute drive back into the center of town and I'd been dreaming of their chicken and waffles since the moment I'd gotten out of bed.

Today was the day I started to get my life back, or at least most of it. I couldn't make my wife rethink the separation and ultimate divorce any more than I could make my own chicken and waffles, but I could work to get myself out of the loft I'd been living in. It didn't mean I'd have the time to fix my truck door, but for the first time in a long time, I saw it as something I *could* do soon. The warehouse and door were just the beginning to fixing what I'd broken six months ago. While that mistake may have ensured the end of my romantic life, it did not sentence me to no life at all. I could still provide for my kids and find happiness doing it.

I pulled onto Main Street and was lucky enough to spot a parking space out front of The Bell. The day really was the beginning of better things, I thought, as I slid my truck into the parallel parking spot. I smiled as my truck fit perfectly between the two sedans.

3

IVY

I pulled into the parking lot behind The Bell and spotted Angie's SUV immediately. I glanced back at Jenny's stocking feet, wet from the dew on the grass that she'd walked through to get to the car. Why she didn't say she'd forgotten her shoes was beyond me.

First Years Preschool was a block away. It didn't make sense to drive all the way home to have to come back when we were already so close and so crunched for time. I resigned myself to picking her up a new pair of boots at the boutique a couple of stores down. They'd be a bit more expensive than I'd usually set aside for shoes, but she needed a pair anyway.

The other option was calling Derick and asking him to run a pair down to us. His loft above the hardware store on Main Street was conveniently close, but I'd be so embarrassed if he knew how the morning had gone. I'd been trying so hard to pull it all together, to do it on my own. I couldn't let him know what a failure I'd become. It would ruin me.

I unbuckled Jenny from her car seat and removed her wet socks. Thankfully, she had a habit of removing them on any car ride and the back seat was riddled in little toddler socks of varying styles and colors. I put on a dirty, but dry pair and hoisted her out of the backseat and onto my hip.

"I can walk, Mo-m!"

"Not without shoes on, you can't."

Inside, the diner was warm, not too busy and smelled of hot coffee and bacon—two of my absolute favorite things. The owner, Madison Bell, sent me a wave and a quick hello before she slipped back into the kitchen. I returned her wave with one of my own. It felt so nice to go places and be known and welcomed. I loved being part of a small town for that very reason. It was the only thing that kept me in town after my separation from Derick.

I slid into the corner booth that Angie had already claimed and sat Jenny on a booster seat opposite me. Angie leaned over and gave me an overly excited hug. "Thank you so much for coming!"

"Of course."

Tessa, The Bell's gorgeous waitress with blonde hair swooped into a haphazard bun handed me a menu with a sincere smile, then slid Jenny some crayons and a Christmas coloring page.

"Welcome to The Bell. Can I get ya somethin' to drink while you look over the menu?"

"Coffee, please." I smiled.

'And for the little one?" She nodded to Jenny.

"Orange Juice?" I asked.

"Chocolate milk," Jenny countered.

"Regular milk," I said with a nod.

Jenny grunted but didn't argue as Tessa jotted down the order.

"Regular milk and coffee. And you, Miss Seegmiller, can I get you a refill on your cappuccino?"

"Yes, please. Two shots," Angie said without looking up from her laptop.

Tessa nodded. "I'll be right back."

"I'll also take a ham and cheese omelet with a side of rye bread."

Tessa paused and turned back to face our table. "Of course. And were you also ready to order?" She looked at me.

"Oh sure. I'll take a cup of oatmeal with a side of fresh fruit."

Tessa pulled out her little notepad and jotted the order down. "And for the little princess?"

"Chocolate chip pancakes!" Jenny said before I had a chance to respond.

Tessa looked at me for approval. I gave it, knowing it wasn't worth the fight I'd get from her if I suggested a healthier option.

"Can I get ya anything else?"

"I think that'll be it." Angie said curtly.

"Thank you." I smiled extra sincere to make up for Angie's lack of manners and Tessa walked away.

Angie cleared her throat and pulled out a stack of papers and flipped her laptop open. Without missing a single beat, she went right to work.

"I was able to pull together what little plans Lexington's design team had sent over"—Angie tapped the laptop screen—"Along with the plans for the last fifteen years of Christmas Celebrations in Holly Springs." She placed her hand on the stack of papers. "We just need to merge these, I guess, and then we'll have some semblance of a Town Christmas Tradition?"

"May I?" I motioned for the laptop. Pulling it in front of me, I scanned the meager notes. "It's not much but it looks like they had some kind of a plan. We just need to make sure it's all where it needs to be at the right time."

Tessa appeared in my peripheral vision and set down my mug of coffee. "Careful, it's hot," she instructed before turning to place Jenny's milk in front of her.

"Thanks," I said.

"No problem. Your food will be just a few more minutes. Can I get you anything else?"

"No, thanks," I said, returning Tessa's smile.

"So?" Angie asked, once again hyperfocused on the task at hand, her eyes glued to the back of her laptop.

"Oh, right. It's not that bad. It looks like they had everything pretty much put together, it's just the last-minute stuff, putting the plans into place and probably making a float for the parade." It was the float that worried me the most. We only had an afternoon to put it all together.

"Well that, and we don't have anyone to be Santa," Angie added.

"What happened to Mr. Erickson being Santa?"

"Uh, he's at Shady Grove Retirement Center after the ice cream incident last month at Fred's Market." Angie's eyebrows rose.

"Oh!' I cringed. "The incident with the ice cream and those goats?"

"Yeah." Angie nodded really slowly.

"I thought they decided it was teenagers playing a prank."

"No, apparently he thought he'd brought the goats into the barn when he went into the market. When he couldn't find a place to milk them, he tried to turn on what he thought was the milking machine or whatever that thing is called and when the soft serve started to spill all over the floor, he tried to clean it up, thinking the goats were leaking freezing milk which is the only thing that almost explains the electric blankets."

"Oh…" I tried not to laugh. "Okay, then. So, no Mr. Erickson."

"No." Angie shook her head, her eyes wide. "He's out this year."

"Who else do we know?"

"Well, I had an idea." Angie laid her half-empty cup of cappuccino on the table and leaned forward.

"Okay." I motioned my hands for her to continue.

"No, it's not really. I mean he doesn't even look like him. I just know he'll do it."

"Who?" I gave her a fierce look.

"C'mon, Ives. The one man who will do anything you ask."

"Fred O'Connor? There's no way. He'll be too busy with his hot sauce truck to do anything else."

"Try again."

The bell on the door dinged as another customer entered or left. I didn't bother to look back and see. But Jenny, who was facing the door, squealed in excitement.

"Speak of the devil." Angie laughed.

I turned to see Derick walk into the diner. Dressed in a pair of jeans and a polo shirt, he walked with confidence, something I hadn't associated with him in years. He'd let his hair grow some, dark unruly curls hanging just past his ears. With his new hairstyle and recently shaven face, he reminded me a lot of the quarterback I'd met and married nearly sixteen years ago. I was shaking the thought from my mind when Angie spoke up.

"Don't you think he'd do it if you asked?"

"Do what? Play Santa?" I asked, surprised.

"Duh!" She said before pulling her cup back to her lips.

"He doesn't do anything I ask."

"He so does, and then some. I thought that's what annoyed you about him."

"No, what annoys me is he thinks I can't do anything on my own. He always tries to step in and fix things and then half the time, they just get screwed up even more."

Angie cringed and her eyes bolted from me to her phone buzzing on the table. "I gotta take this," she said, pulling the phone to her ear as she waved behind me.

"Dad!" Jenny squealed. She jumped off her booster seat and bolted for the door.

Derick's dark unruly hair fell into his face as he scooped Jenny into his arms and hoisted her into the air. He'd always been an amazing father.

"Oh my goodness! I have missed you." Derick kept Jenny in his arms as he squeezed her little body into his chest. "Let me look at you." He pulled her head away with both hands until the two of them were looking eye to eye. "Yep, that's what I thought. You look older."

"I knew it!" Jenny said.

Derick laughed and then looked confused as it seemed to suddenly dawn on him that Jenny was in a diner at eight in the morning. He set her down and looked around a bit. I pulled myself from the corner booth that I'd been leaning out of to watch the little reunion. I wish I could say I was annoyed to see Derick, but the kids loved him so much, it was hard to be angry at anyone who could make them smile so easily.

"Hey!" I didn't push back the smile that had formed during the little reunion I'd just witnessed. "Fancy seeing you here."

"I could say the same."

I nodded and smiled awkwardly. Why did this have to be

awkward? We were married for sixteen years. The separation had only been six months.

"You guys just come for breakfast?" Derick asked, looking down at Jenny. "Oh hey, where are your shoes, princess?"

And there it was. The guilt that so often mounted when I was in his presence. I didn't know for sure that he meant to remind me of my failures, but he always seemed to notice them. Even if he didn't comment, I never really measured up to him in the parenting department.

"Yeah, we were gonna buy new ones, right Jenny? Just after our meeting."

"New shoes?" Derick gave me a nod that was anything but a gesture of approval. "She has four pair at the loft. Do you need me to run some by?"

I took a deep breath. Why did he always have to have that judging tone when it came to stuff like this?

"Mom forgot my shoes at home, cuz she woke up late."

Derick smiled, but didn't say anything.

I wanted to argue but it would be a lie and I couldn't bring myself to do it in front of Jenny. "It was a hectic morning."

"Been there," Derick said. I was surprised by his sudden empathy. Could it be that the separation had shed some light into what my day-to-day was like?

"Why don't you let me run home and grab the extra pair of boots you left in the loft?" he said to Jenny.

"No, it's fine, really," I said, even though letting him grab the shoes would be really helpful.

"Don't be silly, Ives. I'm staying, like two buildings from here. It'll take me ten minutes, tops."

"Fine," I said with a forced smile.

"Do you want me to take Jenny with? Are you in a meeting or something?" Derick glanced back to the booth, no doubt being nosey about who I was with. Did he think it was a date? The thought made me smile for some reason and I covered the traitorous grin with a cough.

"Yeah, if you want to take her with you, that would be great. We just ordered, so we'll be awhile." I answered with intentional vagueness. Him being jealous had a much better feel to it than the possible judgement he might express for me choosing work over family. *Again.*

"How long is a while?"

"At least thirty minutes or so."

And that's when Angie slinked out of the booth and into view, ruining my date scenario entirely.

"Hey, Derick!" Angie said, walking toward us.

"Oh, hi Ange." Derick smiled and I didn't miss the relief I saw on his face as he swung Jenny back and forth in front of him, like she was hanging from real monkey bars. "It's good to see you. How's work going?"

Angie sighed and rolled her eyes dramatically.

"That bad, huh?" He relinquished Jenny's arms and she proceeded to crawl around the dirty floor near his feet, growling like a lion.

"Not for long, your wif—" Angie cleared her throat. "I mean, Ivy's just agreed to work for the mayor and fix the drama in one fell Ivy swoop."

4

DERICK

A blush crept onto Ivy's face and my hand flinched, itching to touch her warm cheeks. Instead, I stiffened my arm and clenched my fingers into a fist.

"You're working for the city now?" My words came out sounding angrier than I'd intended, my frustration misdirected.

"I'm just helping Angie finalize some things for Christmas." Ivy's reddened cheeks faded as her eyes turned icy in defense.

"It's more than that, Ivy. Don't be so humble. The city's party planner bailed last night and left us with a bunch of nonsense for plans and no explanation. Ivy is basically saving the whole town's Christmas!" Angie looked from Ivy and then back to me.

"It's just the tree lighting and the parade. It's not like the city hasn't thrown the same event for the last twenty years. It's practically already planned." Ivy's always been uncomfortable with praise; I wasn't surprised to see her brushing it away.

"It sounds like a busy day. Do you want me to take Jenny

to school this morning? The hardware store can survive opening a few minutes late. We could swing by the loft and grab her shoes on the way."

"No, no," she said, clearly reluctant to accept help from me. Ever since the separation, she'd been reluctant to let me do much of anything, which was funny considering the fact that me not doing things had been one of her big reasons for wanting the separation. I swallowed hard and tried again.

"It's not a problem Ives, seriously. I haven't seen her in nearly a week anyway and you're obviously busy."

Her icy stare softened but she looked sad and I didn't know why.

"It will give us more time to plan," Angie said with optimism.

"Thank you," she said, but it sounded forced.

Tessa came toward us then with a tray full of breakfast. "Hey, Derick," she said, pausing for a moment before dropping off the order she carried. "Did you want me to start something for you?"

"Oh sure. Yeah, I mean." I cleared my throat. "Can I get an order of Chicken and Waffles? Uh, to go?"

What was I supposed to do now? I had planned to sit down and enjoy my victory breakfast, but it seemed odd to sit at a booth away from Jenny and even more weird, possibly, to eat breakfast with my soon-to-be ex-wife during one of her business meetings.

"Don't be silly." Angie interrupted my worried thoughts. "You can join us. The little midget doesn't need to be to school for another hour. You might as well sit down and eat."

5

IVY

Was Angie trying to make this more awkward than it already was?

Derick shot me a nervous look and I could tell he was just as apprehensive. But, he shouldn't have been, and neither should I. If we were going to be separated and inevitably divorced, we could do it as adults. I swallowed my pride and smiled.

"Right. Of course. It would be silly to leave now. You'd have to either come back for Jenny or box up her breakfast too," I said.

Angie nodded and a confused Tessa looked between our now vacant booth and Derick, all the while balancing a tray of breakfast in one hand.

"Okay. If it's not an inconvenience."

"Not at all. In fact, I bet Tessa would like to set the food down sooner than later."

She smiled politely and then followed us to the booth to deliver our food.

Derick twisted and slid Jenny off of his shoulders so she could slip into the booth beside me and start on her plate of pancakes. He took the only empty seat, beside Angie and her mess of papers, across from Jenny and me.

Jenny looked at her food and balled her hands into little fists. The memory of the squashed banana from this morning was all too present in my mind and I did not want pancakes being flung all over Angie's papers.

I pulled her plate out of her reach while I attempted to bribe her. "You better eat up so you can get to preschool; it starts soon." She typically loved preschool and I honestly thought reminding her of it would work.

"I don't wanna go to school today," she whined. "I wanna play with Dad."

Of course she did. Derick was always the fun parent. She had no problem going to school when it was just me she had to leave behind.

I was about to interrupt and tell Jenny she didn't have a choice, when Derick spoke first.

"You have to go to Miss Maisey's class. She's starting the advent calendar today. You don't want to miss the advent calendar."

How did he know that? Why would he know more about our daughter's school than I did? I gave Derick a look and his smile faded.

I must have given him one of my accidental mean faces. I have the hardest time hiding my feelings. It's so frustrating to have everything you think show up on your face. I didn't mean to be rude. He was doing exactly what I would have done. I should have been grateful.

"Right, the advent calendar. That sounds fun," I said encouragingly. "Does she still hand out those little chocolates after?"

Derick nodded, his eyebrows raised as he smiled at Jenny.

Jenny's eyes went wide and she picked up her fork and started to eat.

It wasn't long before Tessa returned with Derick's food, steam billowing off of his chicken and waffles.

"I threw in an extra syrup Derick, just how you like it."

Just how you like it? How did she know how my husband, I mean *Derick* liked his food? The thought stirred up some strange emotions that I did not want to own, so I pushed them down and pulled my cup of coffee to my lips, hoping to hide whatever look was surely betraying me before Derick saw.

"So…" Angie said, cutting through the tension that my mug of coffee couldn't hide. "The Tree lighting. I emailed the grounds crew and they had already been instructed to get the rest of the ornaments on the tree by noon today. The only problem is, the star. Last year's broke when they were disassembling, and I don't know where I'm going to find a three-foot star to top that ginormous tree by dusk."

"I can make you one," Derick said.

I sighed. While he was capable, he was also great at promising and not following through.

"You would do that?" Angie asked.

"No, you don't have to," I said. "I mean, you don't have time anyway, I'm sure." I tried to sound polite but my words came out condescending, almost harsh.

"I actually do have lots of time today. Al said he had things he needed to get done at the hardware store anyhow. After I open, I really don't need to be there. I promise I don't mind. What would the town Christmas tree be if there wasn't a star? I'd consider it an honor."

"Well, that's settled then." Angie smiled as she set her phone back on the table.

"How quick can you have it ready?" I asked apprehensively.

"A three-foot star?"

"Sure." I had no idea how big the star needed to be.

"If I get started right after I drop Jenny off, I think I could have it all pieced together by noon. It won't be amazing, but I think it will do."

"Perfect," Angie said with a smile.

Had I been thrown into a tornado? What in the world was happening? Didn't Angie invite me to help her plan the Christmas Events? Why did I feel like I was getting pushed aside? I took another swig of my coffee and shoved a bite of bacon into my mouth. I was being ridiculous; I just felt like I was being steam rolled again, the same way I'd always felt with Derick in the past.

I swallowed the bacon and took a spoonful of oatmeal and did my best not to speak up. I was annoyed and didn't want it to look like I was angry. I chewed really slowly.

"So, it's really just the float that we will need to work on, Ivy. At least for today."

I swallowed the last bit of oatmeal I'd been mulling around in my mouth. "Great. I have some ideas that have been running through my head since we spoke this morning. Unless you have some already?" I smiled before taking a sip of my recently rewarmed coffee.

"No, no please. I am so out of ideas at this point. My brain is already fried."

"I was thinking, since it's the town's bicentennial, we could do some kind of collage of floats from the past. We could use a lot of the old stuff and piece it together and then at the very end have just a piece of something new. It wouldn't be much work and it would look totally intentional."

"That's not a bad idea," Derick said. His voice held a trace of something. Surprise, maybe? I suddenly felt like my idea was stupid.

"I like it. Will we just have Santa follow up at the end? Or did you want him on the float too?" Angie asked.

"Hmmm… I hadn't thought about that. I was thinking that Mr. Nelson would be on the float and would need to ride, but if we find a younger and more lively Santa, he could essentially walk behind.

"Or ride a horse?" Derick suggested between bites of his waffle, like he was a part of our planning meeting. Hadn't he already done enough as it was?

"Oh, a horse-riding Santa would be cool. Can you imagine? Oh, and what if we had Mrs. Claus riding beside him? And maybe some elves following in the back? They could double as the poop patrol." Angie was way too excited about such a stupid idea.

"Yeah, I guess that could work. If we can find someone to do it. We'd have to find horses too though, and that seems like a bit more work than we have time for."

"I can…" Derick began.

"No, you can't," I countered, my own thoughts betraying my vow to stay civil. "You're already busy with the star. I wouldn't want to overwhelm you with more to do."

"I was just going to say, I can call Mr. Sittoway and see if he's available. I wasn't offering to be Santa or anything."

I saw Angie's face fall a bit.

He'd make a terrible Santa anyway. He wasn't near old enough and the pooch he'd had when we first separated was all but gone. Not to mention, he'd shaved his beard. I was glad I didn't have to openly oppose him taking on the role.

"I'll call Mr. Sittoway," I said. And then to soften the

blunt statement, I added, "That's a great idea. I bet he and his wife would love to be a part of the parade."

Jenny burped beside me, apparently having just finished off her glass of milk.

I sighed. "What do you say?"

"Can I have some chocolate milk now?"

I raised my eyebrows and gave her a look that said she'd guessed wrong.

"Please?"

"I think your mother was referring to your belching there, princess. What should you say after being impolite?"

"Oh… 'scuse me." Jenny giggled.

"That's better." Derick laughed and then waved the waitress over. "Can you get Jenny, here, a refill of chocolate milk?"

"Sure can." She smiled and I didn't miss the way her eyes hovered on Derick before she turned to leave.

"Except," I called, bringing Tessa back. Jenny didn't have chocolate milk. It was two percent. Can you bring her that instead?"

"No fair," Jenny whined.

Derick's mouth pulled into a frown but he refrained from saying anything.

"Of course," Tessa said.

6

DERICK

The rest of the meal was just as awkward; me trying to help Ivy, and her doing her best to refuse. Finally, it was time to get Jenny to school.

"Ooh, you guys better hurry!" Ivy said, looking at her watch. "Preschool starts in fifteen minutes."

After I offered, and Ivy refused to let me help with breakfast, it was my turn to ask for a favor—one I'd been pretty nervous to ask for since I'd offered to take Jenny to school without thinking it through. Mostly because it would sound like me being incapable of helping, but also because I knew it would bring up some issues we hadn't discussed since she'd said the words 'trial separation' and I'd stormed out of the house six months ago.

I wanted to help by taking Jenny to school, but my truck was so full of lumber and supplies that the only available two seats were up front. It wasn't safe for me to drive her without her car seat, nor in the front. I'd have to borrow Ivy's new car. The car she'd bought to replace the one I'd totaled right before the separation.

I mentally prepared myself to tell her about my business,

to let her know that it was the reason I couldn't drive my car and then I opened my mouth.

"So, my truck is…"

"Not working again?" She filled in the blank for me.

"No, it's just…"

"It's fine," she said, her lips forming a thin line that could only be called a smile coming from a librarian or mortician. She reached into her purse. "You can drive Jenny in my car. It's too cold to walk. Just be careful with it, please."

I decided to just accept the offer and not bring up the business. It would sound petty at this point, anyway. I reached for the keys at the same time she moved to hand them to me. When our hands touched, a moment of longing spread up my arms and down my spine. I'd forgotten how soft her hands were. I took a quick short breath and opened my palm for the keys.

"Thank you," I said, but looked away, afraid she'd be able to see the ache in my heart

from the look in my eyes. "I'll bring your car back here after I drop Jen off?"

"Sure. I'll be here with Angie for a bit." She was biting her tongue. She wanted to say more, she wanted to tell me to drive careful, to not repeat what I'd already done when I'd totaled our family car and put our kids in danger. I felt equally grateful for her ability to remain silent and angry over it at the same time. I wished she would share her feelings more; if she did, I may have made different decisions in the past.

"C'mon, Jen," I said, hoisting her from the booth and onto my shoulders before looking back at Ivy. "I'll see you."

"Sounds good," she said, not meeting my eyes. "Listen to your dad, okay? I'll pick you up at noon." She gave Jenny the smile I had been wanting but loved even when it wasn't directed at me.

"Okay, mom."

I turned and headed for the exit, Jenny's legs and sock feet bouncing against my chest.

7

IVY

I pushed my pride down and tried to focus on what I had to do today. I was plenty busy without Derick drama getting in the way. I needed to build an entire float before the kids got out of school at three, for heaven's sake.

Angie's SUV was immaculate and so new. She leased all of her cars and while I sort of thought it was a bad financial decision, I could totally get used to having the newest and nicest of everything.

I slid into her leather seats and the seat heater switched on. She had started the car from inside the diner with her fancy remote start. By the time we got in, the windows were defrosted and the interior already cozy and warm. While Holly Springs hadn't seen the first snowfall of the year yet, it was still plenty cold, which made this little feature that much nicer.

"So, I thought we'd go straight to the warehouse and get started on the float," Angie said, pulling onto Main Street.

"That's a good idea."

"Did you want to call Mr. Sittoway while we drive?" Ange looked at my phone, her smile tight, but knowing.

I did not get along with the Sittoways very well. They'd never know it, but they truly annoyed me. The fact that I had offered to call them only showed how prideful I'd become when it came to Derick. Angie didn't need to say she knew I had been spiteful. Her smile said it for her.

"Shut up." I rolled my eyes and pulled out my phone.

I began searching through my numbers, already knowing what I would find, but hoping somehow I had forgotten that I'd saved one of their phone numbers in my directory. I didn't want to admit that I'd never bothered to put their contact information into my phone.

Angie handed me her phone without saying a word. The number had been pulled up and was ready to dial.

"Thanks," I said, most of my gratitude geared toward the fact that she did not lecture me or give me any sort of a "you're a prideful idiot," speech.

To my dismay, Daisy Sittoway answered after only two rings. They were the nicest, wealthiest and most giving people in town. I had no reason to hate them, which was part of the reason why I did. They were too perfect, and they knew it.

"Hey, Daisy. This is Ivy Winston. How are you?"

"Ivy! What a pleasure. It is so lovely to hear your voice. I am doing well, just putting the last-minute touches on our Christmas display while the kids are away at school."

Of course she was. The sound of her cheery voice was nauseating. I felt guilty for thinking as much. She wasn't a bad person; it was just the clash of our personalities that I found annoying.

"That's great. I was actually calling to see if I could ask a favor of you and Rob."

Just speaking those words made my throat seize. The last thing I wanted was to ever feel like I owed them anything.

"We are always eager to help. What can we do for you this time?"

This time? Seriously, like I'd ever asked them for help in my entire life. Her superiority complex was ridiculous. I fought the urge to hang up the phone.

"Well, it's actually for the town, not me." I tried to distance myself from the favor as much as possible. "You see, it looks like we are in need of a Mr. and Mrs. Claus tonight for the parade."

"Oh, gracious sakes. That's certainly a last-minute request."

"If it isn't something you're capable of doing—"

"Ivy, we would absolutely love to. And of course we can make it work. I'm just surprised that you're asking so late. I thought such details would have been planned months ago. I guess when they put a new party planning company over the town's most revered celebrations, this sort of thing does end up happening." Daisy clicked her tongue.

I wanted so badly to tell her she was wrong, that I was not in charge of the Christmas events, that I had just agreed to fix what the previous company had failed to do. But I knew it would only keep her annoying voice on the phone longer.

"Right, well if you think you two can figure it out, we'd need to know right away. We do have a long list of candidates that we can call if you're not capable," I lied.

"No, no. Rob and I will work it out. What time do we need to be there? Would you like us to wear the costumes I have at home or do you have some for us?"

I turned to Angie for answers.

"5:00 p.m. at the warehouse, and she can wear her own."

I relayed the information and rolled my eyes as Daisy

went on to tell me how she had hand sewn the entire jacket to ensure the embroidery was just right, only then to inform me how lucky the town was to get to see such well-made Santa and Mrs. Claus coats.

"Right, we will all be so grateful." I choked the words out and tried to keep the sarcasm to a bare minimum.

"The horses," Angie urged.

"Also, we were wondering if the two of you could ride in on horseback? We thought it would be a treat for the town to see your beautiful mare and stag at the end of the parade."

"Oh yes, you're right. That's a great idea. You know, your lack of preparation will really turn out in the town's favor tonight. I'll see ya'll at five o'clock."

"Sounds good, Daisy. Thank you." The last thing I wanted to do was to thank such an unpleasant woman. But it was my pride that got me on this phone call to begin with; I couldn't make things worse.

I ended the call and thrust Angie's phone back into her awaiting hand.

That was lovely to listen in on." Angie chuckled.

"Shut up."

We pulled into the lot that housed the town's warehouse, and Angie parked in front of a giant garage-like door. The trailer for the float should be around back, but all the old float decorations were inside.

"Sweet," Angie said turning off the ignition and unbuckling her seat belt.

I noticed we weren't the only car in the lot as I hopped down from the SUV. "Who else is here?"

"I called in some help. Just some of my assistants from the office. "

I pointed to a particularly unique BMW parked to the side of the warehouse.

"Your assistants, uh? Is that what you're calling him now?"

"Pshh, Mr. Handsome just wanted to see me. I don't think he'll stick around too long."

The bay to the warehouse had already been unlocked when Angie pushed a button and the door groaned upward to reveal four people sitting on boxes drinking coffee and chatting.

"Ivy, meet the crew."

The crew was mostly made up of people I'd known all my life. Eric Stansfield was a few grades older than me in school and his wife, Jasmin, had been in my science class two years in a row. James Mason waved enthusiastically. He and I had dated about a week in middle school. It shouldn't have been weird, but now that I was separated, even relationships has far removed as that one felt like they had potential. Finally, Mrs. Samson beamed up at me from her perch on the only chair in the warehouse. Her eyes crinkled with her smile, the white hair adding a touch of innocence that I never would have attributed to her when she was The Pub's most famous shot girl only a few years prior.

"Hey guys!"

They all worked for the city in one way or another so I wasn't entirely surprised to see them. Mostly, I was just grateful they were willing to jump in on a project so last minute.

"Well, let's get started," Angie said. "We're going retro on this one and we need the float finished fast." She pulled out her tablet and set it on a box in the middle of the group. "We're doing a collage of past years' floats, a celebrating-the-past-with-hope-for-the-future type thing. Take a look." She swiped the tablet screen and an image of last year's float popped into view. She proceeded to scan through the rest of the pictures and showed us what each one had looked like.

"So, what I was thinking was taking something from each or even just some of the more memorable ones, pulling those decorations out, if they're still useable, and piecing them together to form some sort of cohesive piece of art," I said.

"Cool," said Andrew. "That's a great idea."

"Since there are six of us, I figure we could each take four years and research a bit, pull out the few items we find meaningful and then bring them to the trailer where we will assemble."

"Great!" Angie said. "Let's do it. It would be awesome if we busted this thing out by noon."

I glanced at my watch. "It's ten-thirty." And then I remembered Mal's presentation. "Oh shoot!" I cringed.

"What?" Angie asked, alarmed.

"I promised Mal that I'd see her report today. It's in half an hour."

"Go. It's fine."

"No, I should stay and see this through."

"You've given your instructions; we can follow them. Just go."

"Are you sure? What kind of party planner skips out right in the beginning?"

"You didn't skip out. You gave us direction. We can gather the supplies. And then when you get back, you can help us put them where they go."

"Okay," I said through clenched teeth. "But only if you think you're okay. I promise I'll hurry back." Every ounce of my body screamed to stay and make sure it turned out how I envisioned.

"We'll be fine dear," Mrs. Samson assured.

I nodded. "I'll hurry. Thanks so much."

"Go!" Angie shooed me with her hands.

With that, I bolted out of the warehouse and into the parking lot, only to remember I didn't have my car.

I turned to head back to ask Angie to borrow hers, feeling totally stupid, when I heard the screeching of tires in the warehouse parking lot.

Who needs to drive that fast in a parking lot? I looked up to see my car. Of course. It was Derick.

He wheeled my car around like some reckless teenager intent on destroying the one possession I'd worked for and called my own after the separation. A car, I might add, that we only needed after he'd wrecked our family car six months ago. I couldn't believe he would drive like that, knowing his carelessness was a huge part of why I'd wanted a break to begin with.

The accident would have been forgivable if it hadn't been combined with the other thoughtless acts; investing our savings without asking then subsequently losing all of our savings, taking the kids out late on school nights to race around empty parking lots to win some fun dad points. If he had thought through that stupid business investment and not been so careless with our savings, if he was only motivated to be the fun dad, we never would have had the fight that split us up. I just wanted to punch him in the face, not work with him all day long!

He parked the car next to Angie's and got out. He smiled and I wanted to slap it off his face. Couldn't he tell I was annoyed?

"Hey Ives..." his voice trailed off as he registered the look I would have expected him to recognize the second he pulled into the parking lot.

"Uh..."

"Do you need to drive like that?" It was so much easier to be mean to him when the kids weren't around. "Seriously."

"Sorry. I was just trying to hurry. I knew how important today was and I was trying to get back in time so you could make it to Mal's presentation."

"You knew about that?" I felt my eyebrows pull together in confusion.

"Yeah. She invited me too. It's for parents. It's practically all she's talked about for the last two weeks."

"Right." I try not to let my anger ease even though he clearly had good intentions. He always had good intentions, it was the lack of follow through or thought that made him so frustrating.

"I'm really sorry. I should have been more careful, especially with my history. I really was just trying to make it on time. After you weren't at the diner, I tried texting to find out where you were. Finally, Angie got back to me and filled me in. I would have been here a lot sooner and not have felt the need to speed if, well, either way, I'm sorry."

Was he groveling? Who was this guy? He never apologized. He didn't just sound apologetic, he sounded sincere. I sighed.

"Your car is amazing, and I'm sure it means a lot to you. I won't drive it again. I uh..."

"It's fine," I said, stopping him. "Thanks for getting the car back to me. I just realized I needed to leave to get to Mal's thing and well, it was actually perfect timing."

His submissive face was immediately replaced with a smile. "Well, should we go?"

"We?" I asked, surprised.

"Well, yeah. I mean, can I have a ride? I don't really have another way there, so I was hoping we'd just go together."

I wanted to roll my eyes, to tell him to find his own way,

but he had tracked me down to make sure I had my car back in time. I was the one who'd left the diner without telling him where we were going. I knew it was unfair when he was only without a ride because he'd chosen to help me out.

"Sure, get in." I held my hand out for keys and he tossed them to me.

Driving to the school was a bit awkward. I realized it was the first time we'd been alone in months. To top it off, we were trapped in a car. I tried to make small talk.

"So, how's the hardware store?"

"It's good. Business is picking up with everyone putting up lights and such. Al thinks he'll be able to put me back on full-time soon."

"That's good." That awful job could barely put food on our table. I hated it so much, but he loved it so I kept my mouth shut for as long as I could.

"Yeah, I know it doesn't pay well," he said, as if reading my mind.

"But you love it." I finished his sentence for him.

"Actually, I think I'm gonna quit soon. I got some plans together to start up my own shop, er, business."

"Oh?" I said, afraid to ask if he'd gotten involved in yet another one of his brother's schemes.

"Not like before, though," he said curtly, his mind obviously going to the same place mine did. "I've been making stuff." He added that last part sheepishly, almost like he was embarrassed. "It started as wall hangings and led to shelves. I made the Sittoway's a desk last week for their daughter and, well, it's just random things like that. But it's fun and I've been making pretty decent money doing it."

It was nothing like him to bet on himself, or to do something that he'd thought about longer than a few minutes. I was speechless. Until I realized he was staring at me, waiting for my response.

"Wow." I finally forced the word out of my mouth. It sounded more surprised than I had intended.

"What?"

"No, it's nothing. I just didn't expect you to, I mean, it's so ambitious."

"You don't think I'm ambitious?"

Again, I could feel his stare on me.

"Uh…" I started to argue but then decided on the truth. "You've worked at the hardware store since high school graduation. You never even applied for another job, or any colleges, for that matter. It wasn't until your brother rolled into town with some grand sales pitch to hock off cattle prods to local farms that you put any interest in making money and even then, you were just investing our savings, not your time or energy. You've always been comfortable with well, what's easy. The one time you decided to help with the yard work, you bought a bunch of tools and a lawn-mower and used them once. You don't typically try new things or do stuff that, well… I just…" I stopped talking, realizing that I was being too honest, and perhaps more cruel than necessary. What he did for a career should have nothing to do with me. I clamped my mouth shut, immediately regretting opening it at all.

"Wow. I didn't realize I was such a failure."

"You're not a failure." I sighed.

"A flake, then…"

"To be honest, a lot of times, you plan to do stuff, but then you don't follow through." There was an awkward pause where I feared I'd really hurt his feelings. I glanced at him looking out the passenger side window. I couldn't see his face but could tell I'd really hit a chord.

"I'm happy for you, though. I hope this business is everything you hope it to be. You're plenty talented," I said, trying to soften what I knew had come off as mean.

I was met with more silence, which was rare coming from Derick. I'd said too much. I typically only spoke so honestly when I was angry at him and now regretted being so blunt.

"I really do think you'll be successful. I'm impressed with how much you've done already. You must really have a passion for it. Perhaps that's what you were waiting for all along. Remember that entertainment center you made us? It was beautiful." I tried again to sound more encouraging.

"Oh yeah; I *did* finish that."

"Yeah, I guess you did." I nodded as my lips pressed into a thin line. My previous words had apparently been way more hurtful than I'd intended.

The rest of the ride to the school was silent, but my mind was reeling. I felt bad for hurting him and his silence just made the feeling worse. I parked in the only open spot left on the side of the road by Holly Springs Elementary.

As I was about to get out, Derick reached over and put his hand on my arm. The sudden warmth sent a calming sensation up my arm and down my spine. I turned and caught Derick's steel gray eyes, serious and sincere as he pulled every ounce of my attention toward him. It was a look I hadn't seen, and a feeling I hadn't felt in years.

"Thanks for being so honest with me. I needed to hear that."

I swallowed. "No problem," I said lamely.

He smiled and then got out of the car.

Mal's presentation was amazing and thorough, of course. That girl was really talented. I wished we could afford to send her to a school that recognized her talents and gave her the opportunity to succeed.

Derick opted to catch a ride back to work with Al from

the hardware store. His son was in the same class as Mal, so he was also there for the presentations. Apparently, that was who he'd planned to ride with before he'd borrowed my car, or, more accurately, before I forgot my car and he'd had to return it.

When I arrived back at the warehouse, I was surprised to see the group had already started on the float. I felt a bit disappointed that I hadn't had more say in the project, but it really was coming together nicely.

"Hey, Ivy! We've saved the best part for you," Angie said with a mischievous smile.

"And that is?"

"The future spot you wanted to have at the end. We have no idea what to put there. We sort of hoped you had a vision for it?"

"I do!" I held back the squeal of excitement that threatened to jump from my throat. "I know just what to do."

8

IVY

It was four o'clock before we finished the float and got it rolled out to Fred's back parking lot. At least we weren't the last float to show up; somehow, the last float to arrive was Fred's hot sauce truck, despite the fact that the silly truck of his sat behind his store year-round.

We finally got everyone in order when my phone rang. It was Mallory. The kids had all congregated at the hardware store by this point and Mal was calling to see if I had time to go ice skating like I'd promised.

My heart sank. I hated disappointing my kids. I felt like I'd been a real jerk all day. I'd said things I regretted, failed to be available for my kids, and now was about to break another promise. "Sorry Mal, the parade starts in two hours. I still have to make sure the lights on the tree work and that the star fits."

"Fine, whatever." Mal's voice was dismissive and I didn't have to see her to know she was rolling her eyes.

"Mal…" I sighed.

I could hear voices on the other end of the phone. It

sounded like Derick was talking and then the line went fuzzy before it cleared again.

"Hey, Ives. I know you've got a lot going on," Derick began. "Let me take the kids ice skating. I'll swing the star on our way back from the pond."

"Are you going to have time to get the kids back to see the parade and the tree lighting?"

"Of course."

"If you're sure, then yes. I'm sure they'd love that."

"We'll go ice skating first and then I'll bring you the star in about an hour and

fifteen."

"Derick, please don't try to do it all. You're going to disappoint somebody. Just—"

"Have some faith, Ives," Derick said, interrupting me. "Let me try to do something and follow through. I'll show you."

Part of me knew he was referencing our conversation earlier and it made me feel guilty; but a more recent and annoyed part saw his comment as a cut to me. *I'd* been the one that had promised to take the kids ice skating and *I* was the one not following through. I took a deep breath and chose to give him the benefit of the doubt. If Derick was going to work on his faults, perhaps it was time I worked on mine.

"Okay. Good luck! I mean, you've got this. Text me when you guys get to Main Street."

The phone call was weird. It was the longest we'd talked in over a year without me fighting the urge to yell at him.

I shoved the phone in my back pocket and turned to Angie who was scaling up one side of the huge Christmas tree that had been placed at the end of Main Street days ago. Thankfully, most of lights had already been strung. It was just the top third that was bare.

"Remind me why we didn't send someone down here earlier to finish with the lights?" I asked Angie through the string of lights I now held in my teeth while I climbed the death trap of a shaky ladder. She nestled her face between the branches of the fir tree, her head poking through them like a cute, little tree animal.

"Because we didn't know the tree wasn't already strung."

"That was stupid. We're going to die up here."

"Well, at least we won't have to put up Derick's star. We can just use you as the angel."

"That's morbid."

"Yeah, probably."

The rest of the light hanging went pretty much the same way until I finally got the phone call from Derick that he was on his way with the star.

Stepping down from that ladder was the best feeling in the world. I shook my head slowly, trying to reorient myself to solid ground, without the swaying and rocking in mid-air. It was like coming off a boat. I rubbed my eyes as I noticed a figure standing at the base of the tree. Was I seeing things?

Standing in front of me, holding the giant star for the top of the tree was a clean-shaven Santa Claus.

"Uh…"

"Hey! The tree looks great," Derick said with a smile.

"What are you wearing?" I ignored his comment and his blasé attitude.

"Yeah. I should have waited to trim up the beard, huh?"

"Right. But why are you dressed like that?"

"Dad's gonna be Santa in the parade!" Harrison chimed in.

"We don't need two Santas."

"No, but you will need one. Mr. Sittoway can't make it."

"But, Daisy said they were good to go."

"Apparently not." Derick cringed. "Rob left Daisy about a week ago. She was in tears when I saw her at the pond."

"Why would she have agreed to ride in the parade if Rob had left? That is so like her. I thought they were the perfect couple. Are you sure?" I paused and looked at him again. And wait, you offered to be her stand in?"

"She was really upset. And I knew you guys were counting on them, so yeah. I offered to help."

"And here you are. Wow!"

"Always the tone of surprise with you." Derick shook his head.

"No, I just…I'm sorry. That was really nice of you."

"Thanks. But that means you'll have to be with the kids during the parade. Will that work?"

"Actually, that may work even better. I need a few kids to stand on the back of the town float. You guys want to do it? The gig comes with glow sticks."

"Woohoo!" Harrison yelled. "Adrianne is going to be so jealous."

"Well, that's why I'm doing this." I laughed and so did Derick. It felt good to genuinely laugh but I paused at the realization that we were doing it *together*. He seemed surprised by it as well. We looked at each other and then despite every cruel thing I'd said or thought today, I smiled at him—a sincere, real smile. He really had been trying to be kind and helpful.

Apprehension fell from Derick's face as his eyes crinkled in a return smile, something I hadn't seen them do in response to me in a long time.

"Great!" Derick said. Turning his attention to the kids, he gave them a hug. "I'll see you guys after the parade. Sorry you'll probably miss Santa putting the ornament on, but at least you'll get to see me riding down the street on that big ol' Clydesdale."

"Santa always puts up the same ornament. We don't care," Mal said.

Derick and I laughed again, this time without the pause of awkwardness.

"Love you guys!" Derick said to the kids with a wink and then off he ran to the other side of Main Street.

"Love y—" I started to say, but stopped myself. It had always been such a habit, I was only acting on instinct. Or, was I? I quickly dismissed the thought. I hadn't said those words to Derick in probably a year. It had been a stressful day, and he had been helpful. It was just me responding to the words. Thank goodness he was already halfway down the block when I'd said it.

Still, Mal heard it. She smiled at me and I cursed myself for giving her false hope.

The parade started without a hitch. I was on the walkie talkie with Angie and the rest of the crew, ensuring that the pacing was going well and that all the businesses had ample time to share their message and hand out whatever favor they'd chosen. My favorite treats were The Bell's goodies. Madison Bell and her boyfriend, along with some other tall handsome stranger walked the length of the parade passing out miniature cake pops shaped like Christmas bells. I'm certain I took more than my fair share, but seriously I hadn't eaten since breakfast. Madison gave me the extras with a kind smile and I almost asked who her extra help was, but the busyness of the parade kept me from prying.

The whole thing was really turning out well.

The hot sauce truck came into view, the song "Feliz Navidad" and Fred's own rendition of "Have a Spicy, Spicy

Christmas" blared as Fred waved enthusiastically from the truck, tossing handfuls of coupons at the crowd.

The Al's Hardware float was lit with extra lights, like something from Disney's electric parade, making me wish we'd done more lights on the city float. Maybe next year. Martha Magdalena's floral shop passed out mistletoe sticks as they walked alongside their float full of poinsettias and pines. When the city float came into view, my heart nearly burst with pride. It was my idea, and there was nothing like seeing something I'd thought of come to life.

When the float passed by, I could clearly see its progression. Starting with the old 1960s Christmas Wreaths they had used, to the 1980s elves, to last year's adorable miniature snowmen. Finally, at the back end were the words, spelled out in block wood letters, "From past stars to present lights, our future is what shines the night," followed by my adorable little kiddos and a couple of their friends waving silver and gold glow sticks.

I would have cried with relief at how nice it turned out had I not been so exhausted. As the town float rolled behind City Hall to where it would park and await deconstruction, I spotted Mrs. and Mr. Claus riding in on their snowy white horses. Derick was now sporting a fake beard that looked totally cheesy, but far more realistic than his clean-shaven face—his far more handsome clean-shaven face. I could see he was smiling even through the beard and when our eyes met, he held my gaze long enough that I wondered, for the second time since our separation, if divorce was possibly *not* our inevitable end.

Mr. and Mrs. Claus arrived at the tree and Daisy, as annoying as she was, looked radiant when Derick helped her down from her horse. She reached back into the saddle and pulled out an ornament. It was a little replica of the North

Pole. They set it on the tree together. For anyone who didn't know the two weren't a couple, or that Daisy was the epitome of all that was evil, they appeared to be the real life, happy pair straight from the North Pole itself.

As they stepped away from the tree, someone from the crowd extended one of the mistletoes sticks to hang over their heads. Derick laughed when he saw it but shook his head. Daisy, however, looked up at him expectantly and the crowd cheered. "Kiss! Kiss! Kiss!" Derick looked back around at the crowd and for a moment, I wondered if he was trying to spot me. Then he shrugged and took Daisy into his arms before dipping her dramatically over his waist.

I felt the bile rise in my throat before the heat hit my cheeks and I turned away. I couldn't believe that just seconds ago, I had thought about not signing those divorce papers. Of all the insensitive things to do; and in front of all our friends and family. I quickly looked around, hoping the kids hadn't returned from the float to see. How could I explain that to them?

The crowd cheered when Derick and Daisy held their hands up and waved. If I wasn't in charge of the evening, I would have bolted for the back of City Hall, picked up the kids and ran straight home. As it was, I was stuck while my still-legal husband kissed the one person I truly despised.

The happy couple took the reins of their horses and proceeded to follow the procession to the back of City Hall. When most of the parade participants had returned to the crowd, including my own kids, the mayor, Nancy Chung, stepped up to the podium, her blue suit and updo hair, making her look like a winter queen as she took the mic in her hands.

"Holly Springs hasn't always been my home, but I hope and pray it will be forever more," she said, and the crowd cheered. "I am so grateful for all the hard work that went on this last year to ensure tonight was so successful. From the amazing design team at Lexington's Designs to the task force at City Hall to each and every citizen who came out tonight and participated.

Her words became background noise to the annoyance, disappointment and anger that raged inside me. Not only had I just witnessed the grossest kiss I'd ever seen, I was getting snubbed by the mayor after dropping everything to make the evening happen. Tonight was only a reality because of me, not Lexington's Designs. I bit my lip and fought back the onslaught of tears that threatened to make me look weak.

I felt a tiny hand reach for mine and clasp tightly around my two middle fingers. I glanced down through glossy eyes and saw Jenny smiling at me, followed quickly by Harrison and Mal clinging to me in some way or the other.

At some point, the lights turned on and the crowd cheered and the Mayor left her post and joined Angie and the rest of City Hall's task force. Music played, a choir sang and it was all probably a very beautiful thing. Heck, it should have been. I had planned it all.

Mal, Jenny, Harrison and I stood in the cold, clear night as the crowd ventured toward the tree and deposited their ornaments before turning and moving away from the tree. Before long, there were only a handful of people left when Jenny tugged on my sleeve.

"Mo-m! Aren't we gonna put up our ornament?"

I had totally forgotten. Every year, as a family, we'd place an ornament on the tree. It was the same one, a handmade ceramic plate with all of our handprints on it. We'd made it just after Jenny was born.

"Of course," I said. As much as I wanted to break off the handprint of a certain insensitive jerk from the rest of the plate, I pulled the thing from my purse and handed it to Mal.

"Why don't you pick the spot this year. Let your brother and sister help put it on."

I stayed back. Although I was willing to let the kids participate, I wasn't exactly in the mood. Instead, I watched as they trekked up to the tree. Just before they reached it, a man in a ragged coat stepped in front of them. I was already so annoyed at the events that had happened in the last thirty minutes, I was about to yell at the guy standing in their way.

Just before I spoke up, he turned to me and smiled. His bright blue eyes and kind face made it impossible for me to voice the anger that had been boiling within. He winked at me. The old man in the dingy coat with the pretty eyes *winked* at me. Then, he turned and placed an ornament on the tree, right beside where the kids were headed.

They looked back at me, confused at the guy who'd just taken the spot they'd scoped out. I smiled and shook my head. It wasn't his fault I'd had an awful day, nor was it his that my kids were left to walk to the tree alone. I hurried up to join them and help them find an open branch.

With heavy shoulders and an empty heart, I pointed to a branch just below the man's ornament and watched as Mal stepped up to hang the plate. I gave her a thumbs up and they all smiled.

"Can we get hot chocolate?" Harrison asked.

As I was about to answer with a 'not tonight', I heard a voice behind me.

"Sure! That sounds great." It was Derick. The sound of his reassuring words brought all my feelings back to the surface in full force. Without thinking, I turned and slapped him in the face.

DERICK

"What was that for?" I rubbed my face, cringing when it just stung more.

"What was that for? Are you kidding me?" Ivy all but yelled as she looked around to see if she had caused a scene.

"Mom!" Mal looked between me and Ivy in shock.

"It's fine, Mal." I motioned with my hands for her to calm down. "I, uh…" I looked around, hoping for some place the kids could go for a minute so Ivy and I could talk. Clearly there was some sort of misunderstanding.

I spotted a line for hot cocoa and reached into my pocket to pull out a twenty-dollar bill. "Mal, why don't you guys go get in line. That hot chocolate looks perfect."

"Mom doesn't like us to go alone in big crowds," Harrison reminded.

Ivy's eyes were slits as she stared at me. "It's fine." She took a deep breath and fished inside her purse to retrieve a credit card. "Take this, and Mal, hold onto Jenny's hand."

I sheepishly put the twenty back into my pocket. Would she ever let me help her?

"Your mom and I will meet you there in just a second." I

reassured the kids when Lizzy looked back at me for approval.

The line went halfway down the street. A wait I would never willingly inflict upon myself, but one look at Ivy told me we would need at least that long to talk. I thought back to the mayor's speech. I had assumed she would be upset by it but upset to the point of slapping me seemed odd.

"Look, Ives," I started, even though her back was still to me as she watched the kids cross the street. "I'm sorry about what the mayor said. It was totally unfair. I can't believe she—"

"Seriously?" Ivy spun around to face me, her eyes wet with tears. "You've got to be kidding me. Listen, I do not want to talk about this. Not after…ugh. Not after tonight."

"I'm sorry. I can't even begin to imagine how you feel. But what does it have to do with me? I didn't write her speech. I didn't undercut today. If anything, I…"

"You what? Offered to help out again and made everything worse? I don't even want to get into this right now. I just need to go home, put on my pajamas and go to bed. I just want to pretend like none of this ever happened."

"I guess I didn't realize I'd only made things worse. I'm sorry. I won't try to help anymore."

"Good." A single tear rolled down her cheek. Even in the midst of her blaming me for her lack of recognition, I had to fight to keep my hand from wiping the tear away. Instead, I stared into her sad eyes, upset and angry that she'd said what she did, but knowing that her words came from a place of pain. I'm not sure what role she thought I had in her night going poorly, but I wanted to clarify it as quickly as possible.

I opened my mouth to speak, to try one more time to understand what had made her so upset, but she cut me off.

"I'll take the kids home. I don't need any of your help."

I closed my mouth and looked down, focusing my attention on where my shoes met the gravel.

"Fine," I said, feeling anger truly surface. I didn't trust myself to speak the words I was feeling anymore. I also didn't want to see her face and the sadness it carried. She knew how much a comment like that stung, and she'd already said it twice in the last two minutes. It shouldn't matter how sad or discouraged she was. Now, she was hurting me, purposefully being cruel. I watched as she turned and stomped off toward the hot chocolate stand.

I shook my head and did my own stomping back to the hardware store, back to my lonely one-bedroom loft.

10

IVY

By the time the kids had finished their hot chocolate, and we were walking up Main Street toward the car, I felt physically and emotionally shot. There really was nothing left in me. Which is why when I saw Angie approaching, I didn't bother questioning her reasoning behind not giving me any credit.

"Ivy! Hey, I've been looking all over for you."

"Couldn't have looked that hard. We've been on Main Street the whole time." I immediately felt bad for my curt response and was about to backtrack when she started talking again.

"Listen, the mayor wrote her speech before she knew you would be helping."

I shook my head. "We can talk about it tomorrow. I really can't do this tonight."

"I'm so sorry, Ivy. Please, let me explain."

"You're the second person who has said sorry tonight, and you did nothing wrong. I'm really just ready to go home." I reached my car and hit the unlock button on the keyless entry, motioning for the kids to pile in. I walked around to the side with Jenny's car seat. Angie followed.

I hoisted Jenny into her seat, her eyelids drooping and her cheeks covered in hot chocolate. I removed her coat and she shivered before I could grab the blanket from the seat next to her.

"Ivy, I mean it." Angie pleaded for my attention. "The mayor sucks at public speaking and just didn't change her speech in time. I told her you were helping. She knew Lexington Designs had backed out. She's just…"

I pulled Jenny's arms through her car seat straps and glanced back to meet Angie's face. I raised my eyebrows waiting for her to finish because I knew she would regardless. If I chose not to speak, she might finish faster.

"You're still getting paid," she added.

"It's seriously fine, Angie. I'm not upset with you. I'm just…" I turned back to finish getting Jenny situated.

"It's not a ton," she said, pressing on. "But I promise you'll get credit, too. I mean it."

I pressed my lips into a thin line as I clicked Jenny's five-point harness into place.

"Look, I know that's not why you did it. You did it to help out," Angie added.

Finally, I turned and spoke in the most controlled, albeit monotone voice I could muster.

"It's fine, Angie. I will be fine. I am not mad at you. I just need to sleep. It's been a really long day."

I wasn't mad at the mayor or at Angie. Heck, I probably wasn't even mad at Derick. I was disappointed in myself for thinking he'd changed, for thinking he might still care for me. I felt like I was grieving my marriage all over again and I just wanted to do it alone.

"Are you sure you're not mad?"

"At you? No. Definitely not mad at you. I just really need to crash." I opened the driver's side door.

"Okay. Can we talk tomorrow?"

"Sure."

"Maybe meet for lunch at The Bell?"

"That sounds great," I said, with zero enthusiasm. I'd do about anything to get out of there before the tears fell.

"I really am sorry, Ivy."

I pulled myself into the SUV and leaned out the door before I closed it. "I know, Ange."

She put her hand on the door to stop me from closing it all the way. "Are you gonna be okay? You don't look so good. Do you want me to drive you home?"

"I'll be fine. Like I said, I just need some sleep. I didn't down four dozen cappuccinos today like somebody I know." I smiled weakly, despite my sour mood.

"Okay," she said, a bit uneasily. She backed away from the car door and let me shut it. She glanced back at the kids in the car and my eyes followed. Jenny was entirely out. Mal sat with her head in her phone and Harrison played with his gum, his eyes drooping.

I started the engine and rolled the window down. I wasn't mad at Angie. I shouldn't take it out on her.

"I gotta go. They have school in the morning, and I need to try and shower before my one-day stink becomes two. I'll be fine after a good night's sleep. And really, Angie, I'm not mad at you at all. It's just been a long day. Thanks for being a good friend."

"All right. Text me when you get home, though? Just so I know you made it."

"Will do." I nodded.

Angie waved, her entire body looking apologetic and worried as I pulled out of Fred's Market and onto Main

Street. I passed Al's Hardware and my heart hit the bottom of my stomach; it was like the day we decided to try the separation out all over again. I should never have let myself believe, even for a moment, that he wanted to change or that he cared for me again.

I managed to stave off the tears until I'd carried Jenny and Harrison into their beds and tucked Mal in.

As I was leaving Mal and Jenny's room, just before I'd turned out the light, Mal stopped me.

"Mom, are you and Dad okay?"

"What, hon?" She'd never asked about mine and Derick's relationship. Even when we separated. Sure, she said it was weird but she'd just kind of accepted it.

"Are you and Dad all right? You slapped him today. What did he do?"

I sighed. This was not a conversation I wanted to have right now, especially with my nine-year-old.

"Nothing, honey. I was being dramatic," I said, even though I really didn't think I was. Derick had shown interest, or I thought he had. He'd at least tried to show me all day how much he had changed. Had he done that just to hurt me?

"Dad and I are just as fine as we always have been. I shouldn't have slapped him, and I will apologize. It's not okay to slap anyone. I'm sorry."

"It's okay. I'd be mad too."

"You would?" My voice rose an octave. Had she somehow managed to see what he'd done? "What would you be mad about?"

"That Dad..." She looked away.

"Dad did what?" I prodded.

"He took your Christmas present back." She said it just above a whisper.

I wasn't aware that Derick had gotten me a present at all,

or that he'd taken it back. But if that helped explain my actions earlier tonight, I'd let my innocent nine-year-old believe it.

"Yeah, it's hard when you lose things. I need to work on that. Get some sleep, okay?" I flicked off the lights and closed her door.

I walked down the hall to my room and into the master bathroom. I turned on the shower and shut the bathroom door. The moment I clicked the door shut, I let myself feel it all over again, let myself drown in it, knowing that tomorrow I would have to suck it up and be a grown up again, one who *didn't* cry.

I leaned against the door, closed my eyes and let the back of my head hit the faux wood of the door before my back slid down until my butt connected with the cold tile floor.

The ache in my chest turned into deep heavy sobs before any tears came. I'd been fighting them back for so long, they seemed to take extra convincing to fall freely.

Once they did, they poured like the shower I'd just turned on. With my head turned up to the ceiling, the tears fell down the sides of my face and pooled in my ears until they trickled down the side of my neck. It didn't matter how annoying it was; it was just another reason I hated today and the way things had turned out.

I was so mad at myself; mad that I'd let the day get away from me, mad that I spent my time with a guy I had already written off, mad that I had let him make me think he wanted me too. I couldn't get the image of him holding Daisy in his arms. I hated the idea of it not being me. As much as Derick annoyed me, as much as he disappointed me, he had never hurt me like this. He had never made me feel so small and stupid and insignificant.

It finally felt like it was truly over. Even though I'd had

the divorce papers drawn up and ready to sign for weeks, I was just following the order that I thought things were supposed to go in. My heart hadn't really been in it until that night, sitting alone in my bathroom, letting myself miss the man I had once loved.

Apparently, *his* heart had been in it though. He had moved on. He had found it all too easy to hold hands with someone else and to kiss her in front of me, in front of all of our friends and neighbors. Why had that been so easy for him? Did he really not care for me at all?

Then I remembered how hard I had worked today, how much time I had put into making things right; with the town, with my family, with Derick. But none of it mattered. *I* didn't matter. I didn't matter because I couldn't do enough or be enough to keep him here. I wasn't perfect enough; even the Mayor couldn't recognize me after all the work I'd done. I was just a doormat for people to step on and over until they got to where they were going.

I was done.

At some point, the tears ran out and by the time I actually made it into the shower, the water was cold. I got in anyway and rinsed off as quickly as possible. I didn't feel like I deserved a warm shower anyway. I felt worthless. I hated that I'd let Derick and the Mayor define my worth that night. I shouldn't ever let him or anyone else do that.

Tomorrow would be different.

After my frigid shower I threw on my bathrobe and climbed into bed. I didn't bother to put on pjs or even brush my teeth. I was too tired, and my eyes begged to close as I fell into my down comforter and gave into exhaustion.

I'd forgotten to set my alarm, so when the phone rang, I bolted upright in a panic. I'd slept in again! I scrambled for my phone to see who it was and how late I'd slept.

It was Angie.

"Hello?" I said, my voice frantic.

"Is everything okay?" she asked.

"Uh…" I glanced around, surprised to see the sun not peeking in through my window. I pulled the phone from my ear and glanced at the clock. It was one thirty in the morning. "Yeah, I'm fine."

"Oh, good. You were supposed to text me," she scolded.

"It's almost two in the morning," I replied.

"Yeah, well I couldn't sleep. You looked awful when we left and then you didn't text. I kept thinking you were stranded on the side of the road somewhere or had fallen off a cliff."

"There are no cliffs in Holly Springs."

"I didn't know where you were."

"I'm fine."

"Okay, sorry if I woke you. I tried texting first."

"It's okay. Thanks for caring."

"I'll let you sleep."

"Sounds good."

"Good night."

"Night."

"Best friends?" she asked, her tone worried.

"Since third grade."

"Since third grade." I could hear the smile in her voice before she hung up.

I looked at my phone and saw at least ten text messages waiting to be read. She must have been really worried. I felt bad for not texting. I quickly set my alarm and threw my phone on the nightstand before curling up in my down comforter and going back to sleep.

The next morning began much smoother than the previous one had. I managed to even beat the kids out of bed.

I made them eggs and toast for breakfast and for Harrison's benefit, a nice berry smoothie.

They ate and I got them off to school without much hassle and zero potato chips.

After dropping Jenny off at preschool, I headed home to really get ready for the day.

Sure, I had showered the night before, but I had gone to bed with wet hair and smeared makeup. When I made it inside, I took one look at the clock and decided I really didn't want to do anything today but be a mom. Yesterday was too fast and I fell too hard. I just needed a day to stay home, do laundry and dishes, and manage the things I could actually control.

I grabbed my phone and called Angie to tell her I couldn't make it to lunch. She seemed worried, but I promised her that I was fine and that we'd meet up tomorrow. The rest of the day was wonderful. I got back into my favorite pair of jeans, threw on one of my old t-shirts and blasted the radio while I cleaned.

For some people a day spent staying home cleaning might sound boring, but for me it was cathartic and helped me feel like I was back in control of my life again. Until my phone rang at twelve thirty.

I cursed when I saw it was the preschool. I was late picking up Jenny. I grabbed my keys and headed out the door as I clicked the accept button on my phone. But they must have given up before I answered.

I quickly dialed back and was put on hold by some very annoying lady. We only lived five minutes from the school and as I pulled up to the drop off/pick up zone I was finally given the privilege of having my call answered.

"Hello, Mrs. Winston?"

"Yes. I'm here."

"Oh, good. We tried to call earlier but got your voicemail. We ended up calling your husband. He's already picked up Jenny. I'm sorry for the confusion."

"You called my uh…it's only been five minutes since I missed your call. How could Derick have gotten here already?"

"No, ma'am. We tried calling at twelve ten and then again at twelve twenty and…"

"And twelve thirty. I only saw the twelve thirty phone call. Okay. Well, thanks."

"No problem. You know if you're going to be late often, we have an after preschool program available for working mothers. You can fill a form out in the front office."

"I'm not going to be late often." I gritted my teeth. Just when I was feeling in control again. "Thanks, though."

"All right then. Have a good day." The overly cheery lady spoke in a sing-song voice.

"Yeah, thanks. You too."

I rolled my eyes, even though no one was there to see me do it. I was so annoyed that the school had called Derick. I mean, I guess they waited awhile to do so. But still, now I had to track him down to get my daughter.

I sat in the front seat of the car and stared at my phone. I reluctantly dialed; of course, he didn't answer. I decided to drive by the hardware store. I assumed that's where he'd taken Jenny, but when I went inside, Al said he hadn't seen him all day. Annoyed, I tried calling again. Thankfully, he answered.

"Hey, Ives. I have Jenny. I just pulled up to the house."

"You took her home?"

"Yeah?" Derick held the word out until it became a question.

"Okay, I'll be there in a second."

I raced home and got out of my car to find Jenny and Derick playing catch in the front yard with nothing other than a balled-up sock.

"Hey!" Derick yelled. "You changed the garage code, so we had to make do with what we had." He laughed at himself and I wanted to smack him. Not for picking up Jenny or being helpful but for how he'd made me feel last night.

"Great," I said with zero enthusiasm.

Derick held the balled-up sock in his hand as he approached. "I didn't think I'd see you until this weekend. How did your night go? Did you get much sleep?"

How dare he ask me if I got enough sleep, after what he'd pulled at the parade.

"I slept fine," I said, my voice still monotone.

"Good. I'm glad." He nodded, and I felt patronized. "I talked to Angie."

"You did what?"

"I was, well, we were both worried—after what the mayor did. I can't believe she snubbed you like that. After all the hard work you put into making the night happen."

Jenny stood on tiptoe at Derick's side. "I'm thirsty," she said, tugging on Derick's jacket.

"Oh, right. Can you let us inside?" Derick asked with a little shrug.

"The garage code is Jenny's birthday." I pointed to the garage keypad.

"Oh." He paused for a second. "Cool."

It used to be our anniversary. I changed it the day he moved out.

"Yeah. It's easy to remember," I said, my tone still unpleasant.

"Yeah, that was a memorable day, wasn't it?" He typed in the digits.

The chugging of the motor blared as the door slowly pulled upward. "That doesn't sound too good, Ives. Do you want me to take a look at it? Sometimes the chain just needs a little oil and…"

"No, I can do it."

"Oh, okay. Do you know where the oil is?"

"No," I admitted after a long pause.

He smiled and I motioned for him to show me.

"My drink!" Jenny whined.

"You can grab a juice box from the fridge. They're in the bottom drawer," I instructed.

Jenny ran inside the house; I was surprised and annoyed that Derick followed. I did the same and bumped right into him when he stopped walking in front of the laundry room door, just to the left of the garage entrance.

"Oops, sorry, Ivy. I always kept the oil in here. It doesn't freeze that way." He reached for the top shelf above the dryer, and without even looking, pulled down a little black plastic bottle of oil.

"Thanks," I said.

"I don't mind putting it on." Derick raised his eyebrows.

"I know. I got it."

"Okay." As he turned to leave the laundry room, he paused and glanced back inside the house. "Wow, the place looks great."

What I wouldn't have given for that compliment a year ago. He never noticed when I cleaned anything before, only when he was missing his stuff—stuff that he'd left out and I had put away in the process of cleaning.

"Yeah, I cleaned." My words were terse and short.

"You seem different today. Are you upset with me? Did I do something? I know last night was rough and all with the mayor, but I can't help feeling like your anger is more at me."

"Seriously? Are you freaking kidding me?" I had lost all the control I'd gained while cleaning. I walked back into the house, passing the laundry room and into the kitchen where Derick now stood and admired the clean house. "You think I'm just mad at the Mayor, or even mad at her at all? I couldn't care less about Mayor Chung and what she does or doesn't do."

"But you are upset." He contorted his face into a confused look.

I glanced to Jenny. while the tv was on in the living room, she had turned her attention to us in the kitchen.

"Now is not the time, Derick," I whispered sharply.

"Then when is?" He placed his hands on the kitchen counter and leaned over it, shaking his head.

"After what you did last night, I'm surprised you want to talk at all." I couldn't even bare to look at him as I said the words.

"What are you talking about?"

"The kiss," I whispered, not wanting Jenny to hear.

"The kiss?" Derick said too loud, his face still confused.

"Please don't make me say it." I shook my head as my eyes tried to focus on the kitchen tile through the threatening tears.

"Whose kiss? *I* didn't kiss anyone."

"No, but Mr. Claus did."

"I'm sure I would know if I or Mr. Claus kissed someone last night!"

11

DERICK

The noise of Jenny's cartoon almost completely drowned out Ivy's voice, but from the sound of it, she was near tears as she spoke. "Yes, you did."

She refused to look up from the ground. She had always been afraid to let anyone see her emotions, but I knew she must be crying.

"I'm pretty certain I would know if I kissed someone, Ivy." I kept my voice steady despite the fact that I wanted to scream at the misunderstanding. "How could you have thought I…I mean, when?"

"At the end of the parade…Daisy." She wasn't even forming complete sentences. I ached to grab her shoulders and make her look at me, but knew it would only make things worse.

"Were you even watching?"

"Yes. Well, not all of it. Most of it."

"Most of it? The crowd held up the mistletoe and I said no."

"Then she looked at you like a long-lost puppy and you dipped her over your waist and…"

I stepped toward Ivy and stood next to her, knowing better than forcing her to look at me, but hoping she'd choose to. "And what?"

"You kissed her." Her eyes glanced up just enough to give me the glare that broke my heart. I'd hurt her. But her lack of faith in me hurt *me*. She believed I was callous and cruel enough to kiss another woman while we were still married?

"I did not." My words were small and too insignificant to repair the pain I saw in her eyes. I felt helpless. "I dipped her over my waist and then pulled her up and spun her around. Our lips were never even close. I would never do something like that."

She sucked in a quick breath and let it out slowly before swiping at her eyes.

"Is that why you were mad last night? And why you've been so weird today?" It suddenly dawned on me that the fact that she was upset shouldn't make me angry; it should give me hope. She was upset because she still cared about who I kissed.

"Well, yeah. I mean, uh, no?"

I fought back the smile that this small ray of hope brought on. "You were jealous," I whispered and immediately felt bad for letting the word slip out.

"I was not jealous. I was angry," she spat back.

"Okay, that's fair." I didn't want her to be angry, even if those feelings came from jealousy. "But, Ives. I would never do that. Not to you, not to the kids. I'm not that guy."

Heat rushed to her cheeks and I fought the instinct to touch her. "I hate this," I said.

"What?"

I almost didn't say it; I almost apologized and walked out. But something inside me kept me standing there, kept me talking. "I hate this whole separation thing. I mean, I understand why we did it. I know I screwed up investing our savings in my brother's hairbrained scheme without asking you first. I realize I didn't ever give you the attention you deserved, that I'd been careless. I get that I didn't appreciate you, that we argued too much to make any progress, that the space was supposed to let us think. But, I still hate it. I miss our family. I miss being a husband. I miss…"

I couldn't say the last thing I missed—the one thing I missed more than anything. I missed her, but I was afraid of what those words would do. Would I scare her off completely? We stood on such a fragile sheet of glass as it was, would my words shatter whatever shaky ground we'd created?

12

IVY

I just stood there and stared at him, suddenly hyper-aware of the divorce papers I'd left lying on the kitchen table in front of him. Part of me wanted to agree that the separation was hard and stupid, but the other part saw the strength I'd gained from it. I had done things I never would have done if we'd stayed together. He had changed, too. He was starting a business; he was grateful for things he'd never even noticed before. The separation had changed us both.

Derick hung his head again. This time, he sat down at the kitchen table. He looked completely defeated. I cringed knowing what lay beneath his now closed eyes. Would he completely give up on us if he saw them? Would I care if he did? Would he think I had given up? I suppose I had. But in that moment, I wanted nothing more than to hide them. I looked away, hoping he'd get up and leave without any more discussion.

"You had them drawn up?" He finally spoke, his voice cracking as his eyes took in the papers laying in front of him.

"I didn't sign them until this morning. After…"

He picked them up, flipping through the pages. "You signed them after you thought I'd kissed someone."

"Well, yeah. Like you wouldn't have done the same."

He looked between me and the papers for a moment, with little emotion until finally his mouth turned into a thin line and he stared right through me.

"No, I wouldn't have." He whispered the words so softly, I couldn't tell if he was sad or angry.

I felt bad, but also annoyed. How did he know what he would have done? I hadn't made him think I'd kissed someone. To be fair, I guess he hadn't either, but he wasn't in my shoes and he didn't know why I had chosen to do what I did. I opened my mouth to argue but was cut short.

"Do you know why I wouldn't have?" He stared on, as if he could see through me.

I shook my head.

"Because this is worth fighting for. I should have fought before now. I'm sorry I didn't." His eyes finally met mine with a determination I don't think I'd ever seen them hold. The air seemed as if it was being sucked from the room as my heart began to pound within my chest.

"Give me some time, Ives." His face was intense. I'd never seen him so determined and resolute. He took a step toward me. "Let me show you that I've changed, that we've changed and that this," he motioned between the two of us, "is worth fighting for."

I knew he meant what he was saying, and I wanted so badly to believe that his words were the prelude to action, but the past sixteen years had taught me otherwise. "How long, Derick? How long are we supposed to wait while we make each other unhappy and do things that hurt each other? It's not fair to drag it on." My hands fell at my sides and I shook my head.

"I won't hurt you, not ever again. I know I have now. I know I've been an idiot and I took you for granted." He sighed deeply and brushed his hand through his dark curly hair. "Give me two weeks. All I am asking is until Christmas. Please? Twelve days to prove to you that I will do anything to make this work. There's still love here, Ivy. You know there is."

"Sometimes love isn't enough," I said. My words sounded callus, but I didn't regret them.

"But if it's real love, it's a start, a solid foundation. If it's love, it can be the reason to make our changes permanent."

His blue-gray eyes bore into mine. He sounded like some love ballad and I wondered if he'd practiced before now. Twelve days couldn't hurt. It seemed less sad to wait until after Christmas to finalize the divorce anyway.

"Fine. I can wait twelve days, but you have to promise that if we both don't feel committed to this one hundred percent at the end, that you'll sign the papers and we can be civil and mature about the whole thing."

"Deal. But you have to try, too."

"I've always—"

"You used to," Derick said, interrupting me. "You haven't tried to make it work since the separation. You've worked on yourself, your business, and the kids and I don't fault you for that. But you wrote me off the day I left the house. You know it, and I know it. Please give me one more chance. Try to see me differently—like you used to."

He may have been right. I truly had given up when he left. But I also invested in myself for the first time in sixteen years. I wasn't sure I knew how to juggle both.

"I'll try," I said honestly.

"If this is going to be a real trial, you have to let me try and win you back."

"What does that even mean?"

"It means if I ask you to go out with me, you have to say yes. If I offer to help, you let me. If I ask for twenty minutes of time, you need to find it in your day to give it to me."

"You couldn't have picked a busier time. With everything going on with the Christmas gala and the kids and their school performances and—"

"Look, I won't make you give up other things to be with me. But twenty minutes a day isn't too much to ask. Just give me a minimum of twenty minutes a day for the next twelve days."

He was right; twenty minutes was less than a lunch break. I could squeeze twenty minutes in for twelve days. But I wasn't going to promise anything more.

"Fine. You have twenty minutes every day. But that's all I can give. It's not just me that needs to give here. I'm not going to agree to twenty minutes if they're spent arguing or are full of broken promises."

"You're right. Speak up, though. Tell me when I'm being an idiot. Be honest with me. You have to tell me what you want. No more biting your tongue and then yelling it at me hours later."

Yikes. I totally did that.

"I may think I've changed, but if I need to fix something, you have to tell me what I'm doing wrong, so I can."

"You don't want to hear all the nagging that goes on in my head."

"I'd rather it be nagging before than anger after I didn't do it right."

"Fine."

He looked up at me, his eyes earnest and pleading, and then I knew why I had to agree to his plan. We deserved one last fight. If we tried one last time, in the end when he signed those papers, I would know we'd done all we could, and I wouldn't feel bad letting it go. Letting *him* go.

Derick looked at his watch. Tomorrow is the fourteenth of December. We can start then. I'll call you in the morning and you can tell me when it's a good time for me to stop by or meet you somewhere.

"Okay." I smiled despite the reluctance I was feeling, reminding myself that this last push for our marriage was the final step we needed to take. I owed him that much. After sixteen years, I owed him twelve days and then I could leave guilt free.

13

DERICK

I pulled my jacket up around my neck as I left the house. The sound of the garage door grinding shut was a cruel reminder that it was no longer my home. I opened the passenger side door and crawled in and over the middle console to the driver's seat.

With the engine running, I blasted the heater. Thankfully, it still worked. While Holly Springs hadn't gotten its first snowfall of the season yet, it was still cold, especially with a window that wouldn't roll up all the way.

The cold was just a reminder of the way I felt inside. What had I just done? Had I really just based the success of my failing marriage on the outcome of my efforts over the next twelve days? I had no idea how I was going to remedy any of our problems in a measly twelve days.

When I pulled up in front of Al's Hardware, I chose not to get out right away. I needed time to think, time to truly flesh out this plan that I'd just convinced my wife, or soon-to-be ex-wife, was going to work. But how was I going to win her back in twenty minutes a day, when I had no idea how to show her it was worth fighting for.

There was a tap at my window. I looked up to see Al, my boss and after years of working together, my mentor and friend.

I rolled down the window.

"Everything all right?" He asked in a somber voice.

"I don't know."

"Well it ain't getting any better out here in the cold. Come in. I've got some tea brewin'."

Without a single word, I turned off the engine and followed Al inside the hardware store, past the register and into the break room.

Al poured me a cup of tea, and him a cup of coffee. The fact that he'd bought a tea kettle and kept my favorite brand on hand, when he himself only drank his coffee black was enough to make me feel like I was almost at home. Almost, but not quite.

I held the tea to my nose and inhaled.

"I think I'm going to lose her for good."

"That's a quick turnaround from last night."

I recapped the misunderstanding and the divorce papers. I even told him about my pathetic attempt to take her on a date and the subsequent result of seeing her for only twenty minutes a day.

"It's a decent start, son. But it certainly can't be your end game."

"Yeah." I sighed.

The silence seemed to engulf the little break room as we both stared absently and sipped at our mugs. Al finally cleared his throat and set his mug on the table.

"You start out with those twenty minutes. You make her see what she's been living without. You need her to want you to stick around longer. You keep track of the time, the first few days, make sure you leave at exactly twenty minutes.

Don't push her. But always try and leave when things are going well. After a couple of days, she's going to stop watching her clock and before you know it, twenty minutes will turn into thirty, and thirty into forty."

"I've only got twelve days, Al. Even forty minutes isn't going to cut it."

"No, no it's not." Al shook his head and took another long slurp from his mug. He swallowed hard and cleared his throat one more time. "When you two reach that hour mark, you ask her if she's hungry, then you take her for some food and the conversation can continue. That's when you ask her to go out with you the following night. Be patient, boy." He seemed to catch the skepticism in my stare. "As patient as you can be in a race. If it's meant to happen, it will."

I finally took a sip of my tea, the amber liquid only lukewarm now as it filled my mouth and slid down my throat.

14

IVY

I got Jenny some more milk and then joined her in the living room to watch whatever mindless cartoon she was enjoying as I tried to think through what in the world I had just agreed to.

How was I going to find twenty minutes every day when I had already agreed to do so much during the next couple of weeks? I still had to finalize all the plans for the Christmas Gala, Mal and Harrison had their Christmas pageant at school, not to mention Jenny's birthday next week.

As I was about to lie down in my pit of worry and despair, I heard a knock at the back door. The only person I knew who ever came to the back door was Angie. I also knew if I didn't get up to let her in, she'd let herself in. I chose the lazier option and waited for her to open the door and come inside.

"Ives?" Angie called as I heard the door click open.

"In here," I yelled back, too mentally exhausted to pull myself from the comfy spot on the couch.

"I tried to call," Angie said as I heard her keys clink against the kitchen counter, and then a thud as she relinquished the giant bag she hauled everywhere.

I didn't remember my phone ringing. I reached into my pocket but found only lint.

"Sorry," I said, sighing. "I must have left my phone in the car when I got home."

"That's not like you. What's going on?" Angie's voice was directly behind me.

"It's nothing. I just…"

Angie came around to face me, blocking the cartoon from my view and forcing me to look at her.

"You're crying," she whispered, as if I didn't know. I didn't bother to wipe the stream of tears away, or lie my way out of explaining why like I normally would. I wasn't even entirely sure why the tears were there.

"I don't know, Ange. It's been a long couple of days. I just don't know what to do anymore."

Angie sat beside me on the couch. Jenny had since moved to the floor to be closer to her show.

Without speaking, Angie put her arm around me. I instinctively let my head fall onto her shoulder. The tears continued to fall, the only sound coming from Jenny's cartoon. No one spoke for a long time. I didn't know what to say; I hadn't let anyone see me cry since I was a kid. Not even when Derick left, after I'd told him I wanted a separation, did I let anyone see my tears. But I'd been caught and there was nothing to be done about it.

I whispered, "I don't think I can do it."

"The Christmas Gala?" Angie asked. "You don't have to. We can figure something else out."

Right. She had no idea what I thought I saw last night or the feelings it had stirred up, or what I had just agreed to.

"No, not the gala." The gala seemed so far off and unimportant at that moment. I uh…" I pulled myself up so that I sat straight and wiped at my eyes before I recounted all of last night's and this afternoon's happenings.

"Oh, Ives!" Angie sighed. I had no idea that was what you saw, or what you were dealing with. I'm so sorry."

"It's okay. I just don't think I can go through with this plan of his. I thought I could, but as he walked out of the house today, I remembered the day he left us, the day he agreed so readily with the separation. I don't know if I have it in me to fight, only to have it end how it did six months ago. He never fought for us before. Why would he now?"

"Because you're worth fighting for. You are! Not just your kids, but you! He was an idiot when he didn't before. But I've seen the change in him since, and I've seen the way he looks at you now."

"He looks at me?"

"Come on. You know he's still into you. He does everything he can to be close to you. I'd say he's *practically* begging for a second chance, but it sounds like this afternoon had *actual* begging in it. What are twelve days going to hurt?"

Angie handed me a tissue from the end table. I wiped at the stream of tears that had finally started to slow. Apparently when you don't allow yourself to cry for a long time, the water gets real backed up or something.

"You don't have to do anything but let him visit you for twenty minutes a day. Just start there and let him try. You might be surprised how easy it really is."

"What if it is easy? What if I let him back in, but nothing has actually changed? I'm afraid I'll lose myself again, that I'll get forgotten."

"Twenty minutes isn't going to take away your identity. You are strong and amazing, and I see you do hard things every day. Letting Derick take up twenty minutes of space in your day is not going to ruin you. You are stronger than that, and besides he's trying to show you he still cares, not punish you."

I closed my eyes. "Twenty minutes. I can do twenty minutes." I chanted the words like a mantra.

"But one thing, Ives."

"What?"

"Be honest with him. Tell him your feelings and what's going on in your head. It'll be a waste of time if you don't."

Darn that Angie. She knew me too well.

The rest of the evening was spent ordering takeout from The Pub, that Angie was sweet enough to pick up for us and vegging out watching tv. By the time the night was over, the kids in bed and Angie gone, I decided Derick's plan likely wasn't going to produce a different outcome than we'd already arrived at. We were just delaying the inevitable. But I had also accepted that it would be easier in the long run to let him try. We'd both be able to walk away knowing we'd given it one last shot.

15

IVY

I sat at the kitchen counter the next day, going over the finances of my party planning/design business. I was surprised at how well things had actually been going. I never thought I would be able to be the type of person who owned her own business, let alone one who was successful at it. But, between all the holiday parties and home redesign projects, this Christmas wasn't going to be as tight as I had originally braced myself for, especially after everything we'd lost when Derick cleaned out our savings.

I entered the most recent income versus expenses into the spreadsheet with a smile. I had never been a part of the finances before Derick's mistake. I wondered for a second how much my involvement would have changed things. Maybe if I had thought myself capable of helping and not just blindly trusting, Derick would have trusted me enough to talk to me before he did what he did.

I shook the thought from my head; there was no point in going over what-ifs now. What happened was over and no amount of thinking about it would change that.

The timer on the stove pulled me from my thoughts. I

clicked save on my work and closed my laptop down before getting up.

I opened the door to the oven, the smell of cinnamon and ginger filling my nostrils at the same time the steam hit my face. As far as past times go, baking wasn't usually my choice, but I'd signed up to bring two dozen baked treats to the school for their post-Christmas performance class party.

I set the cookie sheet on the stove top and used the spatula to lift the little gingerbread men and women off the hot pan to cool on the cooling rack. It was a simple recipe I'd gotten years ago from Derick's mom, but they tasted and smelled like Christmas to me. I had to remind myself to let them cool before tasting them. I also needed to make sure I had at least twenty-four decent looking little men and women for the school before I let myself indulge.

I slid the second sheet of cookies into the warm oven just as my phone buzzed. With the oven closed, I pulled my phone from my pocket. Setting the stove timer for nine minutes with one hand, I used my other to accept call.

"Hello?"

"Ives?"

It was Derick.

"Oh, hey."

"Hey, how are you?"

"I'm fine. How are you?"

"I'm good. I was just calling to see if it would be a good time for me to stop by. I know we have the kids performance in a couple of hours, but I was hoping to get our twenty minutes in before. Uh, that is, if you aren't busy right now."

I looked around the kitchen. It was a mess and I was in the middle of something. I *could* tell him I was too busy to let him come over.

"Ives?"

"Uh, no. I'm not busy. Just baking." I caved, knowing I'd have to do the twenty minutes later if I declined now. I had agreed to the plan and it didn't matter if I felt awkward about it or not.

"Great. I'll be by in a few minutes."

And with that, I had agreed to our first twenty-minute date. I looked down at my clothes. Beneath my flour covered apron were my mismatched pajamas. With a quick glance at the kitchen timer, I decided I had time to race up the stairs and change before it beeped.

I cruised past the entryway, nearly slipping on the hardwood in my socks as I neared the stairs. For nothing more than pride, I wanted to look more put together than I truly was. Pounding up the steps, I raced past Harrison's room and into the master bedroom to skim through my closet. The last few times Derick saw me, I had been wearing a t-shirt and jeans, or a sweatshirt. For whatever reason, I wanted to look more presentable.

One of my favorite winter cardigans hung in the front of my closet. I pulled it off the hanger and paired it with a pair of gray leggings and a blue camisole. Luckily, I had gotten up early enough to do my hair and makeup before sending the kids off to school, so a simple brush through my blonde hair would suffice. I kept my hair down, letting it fall against my shoulders, only tucking it behind my ears as I exited my bedroom and raced back downstairs to the sound of the kitchen timer going off. I hoped it had *just* gone off, but really, I had no way of knowing how long it had been beeping since I was pretty sure it wouldn't have been audible all the way upstairs.

The doorbell rang as I crossed the entryway, and decided it was better to answer it quickly than rush back after pulling the cookies out. I didn't want to make whomever was at the door wait.

I was surprised to see it was Derick. While I knew he was coming over, I hadn't expected him to come to the front door and ring the bell. It seemed weird to have him come over like that. Whenever he came to pick up the kids, he always came to the kitchen door, and very rarely did he knock and wait for it to be answered.

"Hey!" I said, out of breath. "Come in."

"It smells great in here," he said, his head tilting to the sound of the kitchen timer. "Do you need to get that?"

"Yes." I turned around and speed walked toward the beeping oven.

When I opened the oven door, I fought back the swear word that threatened when I smelled the overly cooked dough and saw the dark smoke waft into the room.

It was only a couple of seconds before the kitchen was not only filled with smoke and the sound of the kitchen timer beeping, but the smoke alarm started blaring as well.

I turned on the fan above the oven as Derick worked to open the kitchen windows to air the place out. When the alarm finally stopped, I put my hand to my chest to try and calm the pounding of my heart and settle my nerves.

"Oh, this is my fault," Derick said, taking the blame for something that was so obviously *not* his fault. He surprised me. I'd hardly ever heard him accept ownership of his own mistakes, let alone mine.

Not knowing how to respond and perhaps a little overwhelmed by all the chaos, I opened my mouth and started laughing. The sound reverberated in my chest and throat, and nearly rivaled the volume of the fire alarm. I tried to catch my breath and instead snorted, which only made me laugh all the more.

Derick joined in and it wasn't long before we were both out of breath and sitting on the cool kitchen floor.

"What are we laughing at?" Derick asked when we'd finally quieted down.

I honestly had no idea, so I just shook my head. "You want a cookie?" I laughed a little more.

16

DERICK

I had not heard Ivy laugh like that in years. It was insane and adorable and I could have sat on the kitchen floor for days just laughing with her. Unfortunately, I knew I was on a time restraint and I was trying to follow Al's advice to stick to that twenty-minute rule until she asked me to stay around longer.

"Those dumb cookies were supposed to be for Harrison and Mal's classes after the Christmas performance." Ivy pointed to the pan of burnt gingerbread men before pulling herself up off the floor.

I loved that she was laughing at something like burnt cookies. The old Ivy, *six-months-ago-Ivy*, would have just yelled at everyone and stressed over how imperfect the cookies—and subsequently herself—really were. Her carefree attitude made me want to help her out instead of the usual run-and-hide that used to be my reaction.

"Can I help you clean up?" I offered. "Maybe help you make some more cookies?"

"Oh, I am not making anything else," she said with a smile. "The first batch was a good enough try."

"There's always store bought."

"Yeah." She took the cookie sheet and dumped it, along with the burnt gingerbread, into the sink. "Or even better, I'll call in a favor from Madison Bell and the school will have real baked goods."

"Nice," I said. "You go call her and I'll start on the dishes."

Ivy looked at me like I had just told her I was going to run naked in the snow. Which, when thinking back to our time together, was probably more likely than me doing a single dish or picking anything up. The first thing I'd noticed I needed to change after the separation was my willingness to help out around the house. I honestly hadn't realized how much she had done for me until I was living alone and was forced to do it all myself. Unfortunately, not living in the same house had made it hard to show her that change.

Ivy snuck out of the kitchen to make the phone call while I filled the sink with hot, soapy water. After washing the pan, I got started on the counter tops. The kitchen really wasn't very messy, since Ivy always cleaned as she cooked. When she came back into the kitchen, she smiled.

"Thanks." She looked around at the shining counters and the clean pan.

"No problem. Is Madison available to help out today?"

"No cookies, but she's already baked up some of her delicious raspberry brownies and said I was free to stop on my way to the school to pick them up."

So what do you plan to do with the rest of those gingerbread men there?" I asked with a smile.

"Gingerbread men and women," she corrected, holding up one of the cookies that was shaped to be wearing a skirt and a bow.

"Right. I like it."

"Of course you do. They're delicious." She handed me the cookie and I quickly took a bite.

The rest of the visit went by too quickly. The alarm I'd set to buzz on my phone went off and I wanted so badly to stick around and hang out, to offer to drive to the performance together, but she had given me twenty minutes and I was not going to start on the first day by asking for more.

As I walked out the door, I had the impression that Ivy wasn't ready for me to leave yet either. Or maybe I was just reading into her good mood. Hopefully there was something to Al's plan to get out when things were going good.

"I'll see you at the school in a couple of hours," I said as I stepped off the front porch.

"Sounds good." She smiled, a smile meant for me, a smile I had been wanting for so long. I hoped it would be the first of many.

It wasn't until I neared the hardware store that I remembered the gift I'd gotten for Ivy that Mal had convinced me to return. Looking back on it, a pair of jingle bell earrings was pretty lame. But that didn't mean I couldn't get her a gift at all. Instead of parking on the street outside Al's like I usually would, I cruised on by.

I wasn't needed at the shop until this evening anyway. Instead, I'd look for something more meaningful than a set of jingle bell earrings. Even if it took me the whole twelve days, I'd find something that would show her just how much she meant to me.

17

IVY

Thanks to Madison's brownies, I made it to the kid's Christmas performance on time and with the best brownies I'd ever tasted. Derick was there and the awkwardness I had been nervous about before the whole burnt cookie incident was all but gone. We sat by each other, but he didn't stick around to talk when it was over.

The performance was much quicker than I had anticipated, and it left me the rest of the afternoon to catch up on my design commitments. After a couple of days being consumed by surprise event preparations for the city and thoughts of Derick, I'd nearly forgotten all about the design side of my business. Not only did I have the Gala to plan, and two prior party jobs I'd agreed to execute, I'd also told the library I'd redesign their store front for the holiday.

The Christmas parties were always pretty easy. I'd already scheduled the catering and entertainment for both. It was just getting the place set up and ensuring everyone else did their jobs, but I was concerned about completing the library's window display on time. They'd only hired me a week ago to do a Christmas display in their two front windows. I was so excited to get the job, I hadn't thought about the fact that I should have started on them back in November. Now, I was worried about whether or not they'd even get seen before Christmas was over.

Mrs. Hart, one of the sweet librarians, always seemed to know what was happening in town. She wasn't quite like the other older women though, who knew what was happening and chose to gossip about it. She seemed to be aware just enough to help out where she could. I got the impression she had offered me the job more out of kindness than necessity, especially after realizing the library had already started the window display before I'd shown up. Still, I felt the pressure to get it done sooner rather than later and to do a good job of it.

I drove to the library around the corner and proceeded to carry in my many boxes of supplies. I tried to make most of the decorations I used by hand, or at the very least buy them from a salvage shop or secondhand store. It added a sense of originality and nostalgia that was harder to come by when you bought from the big stores.

As I hung the paper snowflakes made from old newspaper pages and lined the floor with fake snow, I hummed along to Dean Martin crooning Christmas carols through my earbuds to avoid the otherwise cheesy Christmas songs the library had been playing.

I pulled out the angel I'd found at Eddy's Pawn Shop last week and placed it on the top of the colorful Christmas tree I'd built out of children's books before getting to work on the cozy fireplace scene I'd envisioned beneath it, complete with a little mouse family huddled together to read "'Twas the night before Christmas".

If window scenes and home designs were enough to pay the bills, I'd quit the party planning portion of my job in seconds. Unfortunately, in a small town like Holly Springs, the need for interior decorators and store remodelers was even more rare than party planners.

I tried not to think about the money side of things and focus solely on the fun of the project. I glanced out the window through the fake snow of the library at the barren landscape of our little town and realized yet again that we still hadn't seen snow. No wonder it didn't feel quite like Christmas. Despite the wreaths that hung from Main Street's lights, the town Christmas tree and the banner that stretched across the center of town, it really didn't seem like the season began until those white flakes fell.

I turned my gaze upward as far as I could to view the sky, hoping to see some gray clouds rolling in, but found none. When I glanced back to Main Street, I was startled so much, I dropped the cans of fake snow, their aluminum bouncing off the giant library window before tumbling to the rough carpeted floor.

Derick suppressed a smile as he waved, his face attempting apologetic, but really just looking mischievous. What on earth was he doing standing outside the library in the middle of the day?

He mouthed the words, "Looks good," as he gave me a double thumbs up.

I couldn't help but smile at his enthusiasm and felt rude not motioning him inside to say hi.

He looked surprised when I did. He even pointed a finger at his chest and shrugged his shoulders to clarify that I was indeed telling *him* to come in.

Was I really that cruel normally?

I nodded with an exasperated smile which he returned with a genuinely happy one of his own.

I pulled the earbuds out as I saw him approach.

"It looks," he started to say, then glanced around. He cringed before lowering his voice to a whisper. "It looks great!" He leaned in slightly and I caught a hint of his aftershave, a comfortable smell that seemed to fit the family scene we currently stood in.

"I like the little mice!" he said, motioning to the twelve-inch display of the mouse family, complete with a husband and wife surrounded by their three small children.

I hadn't realized until now that I had patterned them to resemble our own family dynamic. It felt silly now and I hoped he didn't read too much into it.

"Thanks. I was hoping to have the Papa mouse read a tiny copy of 'Twas the night before Christmas to the family, but I haven't had the time to make the little book yet. So, no judging its progress just yet."

"I'm sure it will only improve it." He chuckled and then looked at me, his eyes softened around the edges as we both went quiet, the library's cheesy Christmas music suddenly seeming louder.

"What?" I asked, fearful that he was mocking me,

"Nothing. I just can't believe how cool it all looks. You've got a real knack for this."

I felt the blush hit my cheeks and wanted to cover my face in my hands. "Thanks," I said instead.

"Hello, Derick." Mrs. Hart's voice came from behind me. "It's so nice to see you. Did you come to check out some more of the business books? I got a few more in last week."

"No, not today. I was actually just out doing some Christmas shopping and popped in to see the display. It's amazing."

"It is something to look at, isn't it?"

"Truly beautiful," Derick added and for a moment I felt his gaze on me. Was he commenting on more than the display? I shook the thought from my mind. It would not help our situation to start thinking things like that.

"Well, I'll leave you be. It was good to see you two together." Mrs. Hart smiled as she adjusted her purple-rimmed glasses and then turned to walk away, her jingle-bell earrings ringing as she stepped.

I didn't know what the woman meant by that last statement, but she was too old and sweet for me to comment and not sound disrespectful, so I let it slide.

"Well, I should get going. I have more Christmas shopping to do."

My heart seemed to fall. The sudden shift in my mood made me confused. I had already squeezed in twenty minutes with this guy, I was busy and did not owe him more than we agreed to. So why, as I watched him exit those library doors, did I suddenly feel like something was missing?

After finishing up at the library, I drove around the block to pick Jenny up from preschool. She came bounding out of the classroom with a smile so big, I couldn't help but return it with one of my own.

"You came to get me today, mom!" She seemed surprised.

"Yeah, like every other day."

"Well, except yesterday when you forgot," she corrected.

The guilt washed over me and I felt my smile fade.

"I didn't forget. I was just running a little late."

"I'm glad you ran early today."

"Me too."

"But Dad was fun too. Maybe next time you can both pick me up?" She wrapped her little arms around my neck, and I felt her sweet chubby cheeks against mine. She was so innocent and easily accepting. I adored her for that and wished, for a moment, that I could be more like her.

On the way out of First Years Preschool, she caught site of the town Christmas tree. As I tried to steer us in the opposite direction, she tugged my arm toward the giant pine in front of City Hall.

"Can we look? I want to see our ornament." Her big blue eyes pleaded with me. How could I say no? It wouldn't hurt to stop for a minute.

We approached the giant tree and I tried to remember where we placed our family plaque when Jenny squealed. "I see it!" She jumped up and down until we reached the spot it where it hung.

"Do you think Dad will be able to hang it with us next time?"

The fact that her dad was no longer living with us and that him and I had fought in front of her the other day didn't seem to register as any sort of big deal. She adored him and me and saw no reason we shouldn't all be together. Once again, I wished for that sort of simplicity in my life. I reached down to touch our little family heirloom and saw each of our handprints in the concrete slab, each of our names written below. It was one of the biggest ornaments on the tree, but not the biggest. I wondered if we would even use it next year, or if we'd need to find a replacement.

As I pulled my hand away, a speck of light reflected off the hourglass ornament that hung just above ours. I remembered the strange man from the parade who had put it there. I extended my hand and cupped the ornament in it. It was beautiful. The sand dripped as if it had recently been turned over. I looked around but didn't see anyone near.

It was mesmerizing as it fell grain by grain, as if watching it slowed down time itself. I was reluctant to look away;

slowing time was exactly what I needed. I needed everything to just stop so I could think. I needed time to make the right decisions. Without thinking, I wished for that. I wished that time would slow, that I could know the best thing to do for me and my family, for my kids. I pleaded for time.

A small hand clasped mine and started to tug me in the opposite direction again. I willed myself to look away.

"C'mon, Mom," Jenny whined. "Let's go! It's cold."

My phone buzzed in my pocket, a reminder that life doesn't just stop, and time doesn't stand still for anyone, even when big choices need to be made. Things still needed to get done and I was the one who needed to do them.

As we walked back to the car, I pulled the phone from my pocket and read the text that had just come in. It was Madison Bell, checking in about Jenny's birthday cake. I'd hired her weeks ago to create a princess cake that was going to make Jenny over the moon happy.

CAKE IS NEARLY DONE 😊 , her text read. **YOU CAN BRING THE TOPPER BY WHENEVER YOU'RE READY.**

"Your cake's almost ready," I told Jenny as we neared the car.

"Can we pick it up today?"

"I think so. We'll be needing it tomorrow, so I imagine we can bring it home today sometime."

Jenny climbed into her car seat and I proceeded to help her buckle in, a task she was capable of doing on her own, but I still enjoyed helping.

"You want to go look at it now?" I asked.

"Yeah! Can we?"

"Heck yeah, we can." I smiled as I pulled onto Main Street and made my way to The Bell.

DERICK

The next day was Jenny's birthday and Ivy and I had agreed that we would celebrate it together, long before she even agreed to the twenty-minute plan.

After a long morning spent in the warehouse working on a custom-built dining room set, I took a quick shower, happy to get the sawdust and varnish off my skin. I towel dried my hair and stood in front of the mirror, debating on whether shaving was a necessity. Running my hand over my mouth and jaw, I had to admit I was looking a little scruffy, but Ivy liked a little facial hair, as long as it didn't look like a truck driver on the last stretch of his trip.

I tilted my head back and forth in the mirror, trying to decide if what I had growing on my face was more Ryan Gosling or Shady Joe from the rest stop in Reno. I hadn't been that concerned about my appearance since high school and suddenly felt anxious about the entire party.

I began to wonder if the party was going to count as our twenty minutes of time or if she was expecting an extra twenty minutes later or even earlier? Had I already screwed things up?

I hated all the uncertainty of single life. What I wouldn't give to just go home, and let Ivy tell me when I should shave and what I should wear to the party. It was funny how that sort of stuff would have gotten on my nerves before the separation, but I craved it now that it was gone.

I settled on leaving the beard but trimmed up my neck and around my ears a bit. I wasn't one of those guys who typically did trimming of any kind; it was usually an all or none situation, but I only had a small window of opportunity and needed to optimize as much as possible.

The birthday party was mostly a bunch of four-year-old kids and a couple of parents who had decided to stick around, plus a handful of cousins and Ivy's mom.

I was surprised by the elaborate decorations and the amazing Rapunzel cake that sat in the middle of the table. It seemed more elaborate than the company required, and made me grateful I had opted for trimming my beard.

Then I spotted Ivy on the ladder near the cake. She stretched her arms out to hang a happy birthday banner while Jenny jumped and clapped at the base of the stool. I realized then, that the decorations weren't for anyone but Jenny. Ivy loved to decorate. She was good at it and this was her way of showing Jenny how much she loved her. She was such a good mom.

The party went great. Ivy had gone all out with a sandwich bar, a scavenger hunt, a pinata, and finally homemade ice cream to go with the elaborate Rapunzel cake that looked more like a work of art than something to eat.

After cake and ice cream, Jenny opened her presents and it wasn't long before her and most of the kids ended up in princess costumes jumping on the trampoline in the backyard.

I tried to help as often as it looked like an extra pair of hands were needed, but Ivy had put so much into the planning of the party that everything seemed to just happen effortlessly. Finally, while Ivy was busy handing out the party favors to the kids as their parents came to pick them up, I saw the mess in the kitchen and got to work.

"I wasn't aware you even knew where the kitchen was." I tried not to tense at the sound of my mother-in-law's voice.

I swallowed hard before turning around to give her my best—possibly most rehearsed—smile. "Marjorie. It's good to see you."

"I'm sure." Her lips pressed into a thin line. "It's been a while. How are things at the hardware store?" I didn't miss the demeaning tone in her voice.

"Things at Al's are great." No way was I telling her about my new business. It was none of hers and she would only find a way to make me feel bad about it.

"Great. Well. You can go sit on the couch and watch your game or—"

"I actually came in to help," I said, clenching my jaw so I didn't accidentally say any of the other thoughts I had in my head.

I'd always been afraid of Ivy's mom, to the point that I would typically just do whatever she said, but not anymore. Especially if it meant the detriment of my chances with my wife.

"Hmmm." Her lips returned to the thin line of disappointment. She shrugged and turned to the sink of soapy water and I went back to gathering paper plates, napkins and all the other miscellaneous garbage. I'd told Ivy I was going to be more helpful and I'd meant every word of it.

As I gathered the last of the garbage, I tied it all together and made my way outside to the dumpster. The noise of the party seemed to have died down as I walked to the back of the house. Even the trampoline was only occupied by our own children. They hardly noticed me as I walked by; they were laughing and jumping so much, I doubted they would have noticed if Santa was taking out the garbage.

When I reentered the kitchen, Ivy had joined her mom and was wiping down the countertops. Based on their conversation, neither of them had heard me come in.

"I just don't know why you even invited him," Marjorie chided as she rinsed off the last few large bowls.

"He's her father, mom."

"He left her when he left you."

I opened my mouth to defend myself. I did not leave Ivy in the way Marjorie was claiming, nor did I abandon my children. But before I could say anything, Ivy responded.

"I asked him to leave."

"He's just like your father," Marjorie retorted.

"No, dad left and never came back. He abandoned his family. Derick has always been a good father. He showed up today. Don't ever compare the two."

Realizing this conversation was probably one I shouldn't be around for, I took a step back, hoping to sneak out. My foot hit the barstool near the counter and the stool's legs dragged against the floor.

Both women paused and looked back at me.

I didn't have words, just an awkward smile that crept onto my face.

"Speak of the devil," Marjorie said in a mock whisper.

Ivy looked embarrassed.

"Can I get you something to drink or eat, Derick?" Ivy said, ignoring her mother.

"Oh, no. I came in to help, not make more of a mess."

"I suppose there's a first for everything," the demon woman said, but after her comment about me abandoning my wife and children, her little jab was barely felt.

Ivy took a deep breath and gave me a kind smile, one I hadn't seen directed at me in a long time. "Mom, I appreciate your help, but it's getting late. I think Derick and I can handle things from here."

The demon paused in the middle of drying her last bowl. "If that's how you feel."

"I'll walk you out," Ivy said with a smile. "I don't want you driving home after dark. It isn't safe."

Marjorie dried her hands on the dish towel and turned to exit the kitchen. Ivy mouthed an "I'm sorry" to me as she followed her mother to the door.

I waited quietly and admittedly tried to eavesdrop, but whatever the ladies were saying was too quiet to be heard in the kitchen. Wanting to show that I was really trying to help, I went to the sink and finished up Marjorie's chore.

"Now," Ivy said as she pushed the stool I'd shoved back beneath the counter. "Can I get you something to drink? You're probably thirsty after all the work you've been doing around here."

I smiled before she turned around. She'd noticed.

"Thanks," I said. "You don't have to though. I mean, this was much longer than twenty minutes."

"Shut up." She playfully hit me in the arm. "It's the least I can do after all you've done today. Sit down. This kitchen is cleaner than it's been in weeks."

"Well, I did take that garbage all the way to the outside bin."

Ivy's smile was relaxed, and it prompted me to sit and relax myself.

"Peppermint tea sound okay?" she asked, pulling down the box of tea from the cupboard.

"Sounds great."

She brought over the steaming mug and set it in front of

me and then turned back toward the sink to put the bowls away.

"Aren't you going to join me?" I asked, and then immediately regretted it. I didn't want her to feel obligated.

"Oh, uh...sure."

Al's advice about making her want to be with me for more than twenty minutes came to mind. I glanced at the clock. 7:45. I would make up an excuse to leave at 8:05.

She poured herself a cup of tea and sat at the table with me. Her small hands seemed dwarfed by the oversized mug as she steeped her tea. We sat in silence for a minute and watched the kids huddle around the animated Christmas show they were watching in the living room. *Rudolph the Red-Nosed Reindeer* played and I smiled as Harrison lay on his stomach, his legs bent up in the air, wiggling to the beat of the song.

"Do you remember those shows when we were kids?" Ivy asked.

"Yeah. The animation has improved, hasn't it?"

"Songs are the same though." She chuckled.

A few more minutes of surface level conversation passed, and I was beginning to worry that we really would never reconnect.

"I'm sorry about my mom." Ivy surprised me with a real comment.

"Oh, it's okay." I wasn't sure what to say. Her mom had never been kind to me, but Ivy had also never apologized for it. I'd always assumed she either didn't notice or didn't care.

"She's always been uptight around men. It really has nothing to do with you. It never did, really. She's just never been very trusting of men, not that I've ever known. It probably has something to do with the man who may have been called my father had he stuck around long enough to see me out of diapers."

I hadn't thought about that perspective before. I'd just always been annoyed by the woman. I nodded. "It may have *something* to do with me now, though." I decided to keep my words real; it was better than wasting our twenty minutes being superficial. "I mean, technically, from her perspective, it may look like I left, just like your dad."

Ivy's eyes went wide. Had I struck a nerve? I regretted my honesty immediately.

"I mean, she's fine. I've actually gotten to enjoy our little back and forth." I backpedaled.

"No you haven't." Ivy laughed awkwardly but it seemed to relieve some of the tension I'd just put between us. "She's horrible to you."

"Yeah, she's never been too fond of me. Although, tonight her words were a bit more biting than in the past."

Silence followed. It felt like hours and I caught myself watching the time, wondering if maybe twenty minutes was too long.

"I'm sorry, Derick," Ivy finally said. "You leaving was nothing like what my father did." She said *father* with air quotes. "I asked you to go, and you did what I asked. Mom doesn't know all the details."

"Still, maybe I left too willingly."

Ivy just nodded. I wished I knew what she was thinking. Did she agree that I should have fought to stay? Or was my comment too bold for her to respond? My watch buzzed. Our twenty minutes were up. What a horrible ending to our conversation. I'd hoped to end on a happy note. But maybe it was better to go now before I said anything I'd regret later. Marjorie really put me in a mood I wasn't prepared to handle, at least not with an audience.

"Well, I think our time is up. I should get going."

"Oh. Yeah. You're right."

I stood and Ivy did the same. I gave the kids hugs and told them goodnight.

"Love you, Daddy!" Jenny said, wrapping her arms around my legs. I bent down and kissed her cheek. "Happy Birthday, Princess."

I got a "Night, Dad," from Harrison and a little side hug from Mallory.

"Did you still want me to take them next week after their Christmas performance?"

"If that works for you. I've got the Lodge Christmas party the next day. It would be nice to know they were in good hands while I worked."

"Perfect. I'll plan on it."

She walked me to the door. I grabbed my jacket off the coat rack and slipped it on as I stepped outside.

"It was a great party, Ives." I wanted to tell her what a great job she had done, but was

worried it would come out sounding stupid or insincere, so I kept it general.

"Thanks for coming. Jenny was so happy you made it."

We stood at the door, her inside the house and me on the front porch. Images of our early

dating came to mind; me, dropping her off and trying to kiss her; her, letting me. I stood there and stared at her for probably way longer than was comfortable, but I couldn't convince my legs to move.

My hand flinched at my side as I involuntarily started to reach for her.

"I'll see you tomorrow," I said, forcing my hand into a fist at my side before burying it in my jacket pocket.

"Sounds good. Drive safe. It's supposed to snow tonight."

"It's about time," I said with a laugh. "And I will."

"Goodnight, Derick."

"Goodnight, Ivy." I turned and walked to my truck, the chilly air a perfect companion to

the cold emptiness I was about sit with after I left her for another night.

IVY

I shut the front door but watched Derick drive away from the front window in the living room. My mind reeled around our conversation and his overall change in attitude. He was helpful and kind and aware. And what was that comment about him not fighting to stay? I'd never said anything to him about that. Did he regret not fighting to stick around?

"Moooom!" Harrison whined from the other room. "Mal won't give me the remote and
it's my turn to pick something."

I closed my eyes and took a deep breath. It was bedtime. I just needed to get them in bed and then I could think through the night's events and the meaning behind Derick's comments and actions.

After a little whining, a tantrum or two and some bribing on my part, the kids were in
their beds and I was left alone to think. Unfortunately, the moment my butt hit the living room
sofa, my eyes closed and the alone time I'd promised myself to think and plan out my day and

all my options faded into my dreams.

I got the phone call from Angie the next morning, fortunately not as early as her previous early morning calls. I was grateful that I had the opportunity to start my Sunday slow, especially with the knowledge of how busy my evening would be with the Church Nativity and the children's Christmas performance.

"Ivy!" Angie said with a tinge of excitement in her voice that I hadn't heard in a long time.

"Hey, Ange. What's going on?"

"I just got a call from the mayor. She loved the parade and is insisting that we use the same team we assembled for it on the gala. Are you able to meet tomorrow afternoon with the team to share your plans with everyone and get things rolling?"

Her enthusiasm was over the top. She was trying to make this sound better than it was.

"What's the catch, Angie?"

"What? No. There's not a catch."

"Angie."

"It's nothing, really. Just that the former design team that the mayor had hired is also going to be working on it. Well, sort of."

"I don't need a pity job, Angie." I was more than happy to give up the whole gala gig. It's not like I didn't have enough on my plate.

"It's not like that. Actually, it's kind of the other way around. The mayor hired the former party planning company because her cousin was one of the owners. When their company went bankrupt, she lost her job. Letting her and a couple of her team join yours would actually be a pity job for them, not you."

I groaned inwardly, surprised by and impressed by my restraint. "I guess more hands wouldn't hurt."

"Great. I knew you'd be cool with it. And the commission would be the same for you, so you don't need to worry about splitting the money up between more team members. The mayor promised you'd get the same pay as you'd agreed on before."

I hadn't even considered the money portion of it all. "Okay, good to know. Will they all be at the meeting tomorrow?"

"Yes. Can you meet Monday afternoon around one at City Hall?"

"I think so. As long as I can get someone to watch Jenny."

"Great. Thanks so much, Ivy. You're a lifesaver."

"No problem."

We hung up and I immediately dialed Derick's number.

"Hello?" His voice sounded confused. He probably thought I'd called by accident. It was rare that I ever called on one of his days off from having the kids.

"Hey. How's it going?"

"Good. How are you?"

"I'm fine but could use a small favor."

"Yeah, shoot."

"Would you be available to take the Jenny around one on

Monday, maybe pick her up from preschool? I had a surprise meeting come up for the gala project."

There was a long silence where I wondered if maybe I'd become a little too comfortable with Derick's recent reliability. I started to regret calling him at all. I should have just stuck to who I knew would help out at the last minute. I should have called my mom.

Finally, he cleared his throat. "Yeah, I can pick her up, and we can hang out at the house in case the older two get out of school before you're done."

I sighed with relief. I knew he would take them, but something about asking him still

made me nervous.

"It was for tomorrow, right?" I swore I'd heard his voice crack a little. I almost laughed but decided against it.

Instead I settled with a simple, "Yeah. Tomorrow at one."

"Uh, well do you have plans for tonight?"

"I, uh..." He'd caught me off guard. Was he asking me out?

"You aren't working or anything, are you?"

"No, not really. I don't have another party planning gig until next weekend."

He cleared his throat again. "Can I arrange a sitter for the kids? I'd like to take you out to dinner. While we're there, you can tell me the things you want from me, tell me what I've been doing wrong, and I'll listen. I think it will be good to get it all out."

I wanted to believe that twelve days could change the destructive path our marriage had been on for years, but I knew those divorce papers were the inevitable end. But what could one date hurt? If it gave him more closure, if it allowed him to understand where I was coming from, that would be worth it.

"Okay," I agreed.

"Great. I'll pick you up at seven?" His words were a question and I realized he was asking me out, still giving me a choice.

"All right." I smiled despite the apprehension I felt. I hoped and prayed I was doing the right thing, because right now it really felt like I might just be leading him on.

20

IVY

It was six thirty when the babysitter showed up. It was the teenage girl from down the street, Lucy. She used to babysit all the time. She'd been my favorite babysitter until she got 'too old' and had gotten a real job and never had time anymore.

Mal insisted numerous times that she was old enough to watch the kids without help. I reminded her that Lucy was not there to help, but there to watch her as well and that it would be nice if she listened and got ready for bed when Lucy asked.

At 7:00 p.m. on the dot, the doorbell rang. Mal's smile that I had destroyed when telling her that she was being babysat instantly returned when she saw her dad standing on the doorstep with a bouquet of lilies in his hand, my favorite flower.

I smiled and invited him in.

"Thank you," I said as I took them from him. "I should probably put these in water really quick."

"I can do it for you, Mrs. Winston," Lucy chimed in. Man, I loved her. "You get going. Have fun." The girl spoke like she was my mother sending me off to prom. It was almost annoying but I chose to find humor in it and returned her encouragement with a smile.

"Okay, then. Mal, Jenny, Harrison!" I called. "I'll be back later tonight. Listen to Lucy and please, please be good." They gave Derick and I both hugs. I didn't miss how much Derick's expression changed when his kids wrapped their arms around him. He loved them, and I hated that our separation took them from him so often.

"See you guys later," he said. A huge part of me felt sorry that he wouldn't be able to see them tonight like I would. He'd have to wait until the weekend when he had his visits. Divorce wasn't always fair to everyone, I reminded myself, but a lousy marriage full of fighting and cruelty was never fair.

Derick led me to his truck. I was about to reach my hand into the window to open the broken door from the inside, when he stepped in front of me and with a click of the outside handle opened the door and gestured for me to get in.

"Ooh, you fixed it."

"It was nothing." He smiled before walking around to his side of the car and getting in.

"So, where are we going?" I asked as the engine started. The musty smell of the heater filled the cab, reminding me of other cool night drives in his truck.

"I thought we'd have dinner at The Pub."

"Good choice." It was really the only option in Holly Springs, but I did like their food.

"And then I thought we would go to the new art shop that opened last week."

"What are we going to do at an art shop?" I asked, apprehensive. I didn't usually like trying new things.

"You'll see. It'll be fun. I promise."

"Okay," I said.

The Pub was packed, but that was no surprise. Even on Sunday nights, they stayed busy. As we reached the hostess, Derick whispered something in her ear and she nodded with a smile.

"Follow me," she said. She escorted us through the throng of waiting, hungry people to a booth in the back corner.

"How in the world did you do that?" I asked. "I didn't think they took reservations."

"Not normally," Derick said. "But I know a guy."

I laughed. It was a weird, free sound that I hadn't heard in a while.

Derick smiled as the waiter approached, gave us both menus and took our drink orders.

"So," I said when the silence started to become uncomfortable.

"Yeah, so I thought we could talk a little about our agreement. You know, make sure we're both on the same page. Have you thought about what sort of things you would have me do differently than I did before?"

The question caught me off guard. I had assumed this little experiment was more to get me to forget his mistakes than it was to actually help repair them.

I surprised myself even more when I said, "I have, actually."

"And?" He cleared his throat.

I took a deep breath. I'd said I would try to be honest. I owed him honesty. I'd thought of these things long before I even mentioned the separation, so it wasn't hard for them to come to mind when he asked. "Well, it's really only three things."

"And they are?"

I nodded, deciding to just say it and get it out there. "First, I want you to take me seriously."

"What?" His eyebrows pulled together. "I do."

"No, you may think you do. But you don't or at least I don't feel like you do."

"Okay, how can I take you seriously?"

"For starters, when I say something that you don't agree with, like a political opinion or maybe something to do with the kids, I want you to think about my point of view before brushing it off."

Derick looked at me, his eyes suddenly sad. "You felt like I was brushing you off before?"

"Yes," I said matter-of-factly.

"I am so sorry."

"Thank you." I didn't know what else to say.

"What else?" he prompted.

"This sort of goes along with the first request, but when I'm angry or upset, I want you to validate me. I don't care if you're angry or upset alongside me, I just want you to care because it bothers me."

"That is a valid request." He nodded. "I will definitely work on that."

"Thank you."

"And the last thing."

"You have to follow through."

"I thought that might be one."

"Don't patronize, please." I heard the sadness in my voice and immediately felt more vulnerable than I was ready for.

"I'm not. After the other day when you told me how I don't follow through on things, I thought about it a lot and you're absolutely right. I'm a flake. I hate it and it hurt to realize it, but it's true. It's the first thing I want to change."

"Okay," I said, feeling a tinge of guilt at my blunt

honesty.

"Is it just those three?" he asked earnestly.

"I think so."

"All right. But if you think of more, you have to promise to voice them. The one thing I request is that you do not let it fester until you have to yell it at me." His face was serious.

"Okay. I'll try really hard," I said.

"Sweet. Now that *that* is out of the way, what are you going to eat?"

I wanted to laugh at the nonchalance of it all. I had just told him things that had been bothering me for years—hurtful things. But we'd said them with such calm and matter-of-factness, it practically felt natural to move right into the mundane of what we were going to eat.

Dinner went well. I was surprised how much we had to talk about. Our conversation began around the kids but slowly transformed into what he was doing at the hardware store and how far he was progressing in his business plans. I was surprised to learn that he'd already been selling quite a few pieces to people around town, enough to put a deposit on a little warehouse he could use as a wood shop to create more.

"Have you filed for a business license yet?"

"Last week," he said with a smile.

"Wow. I really am impressed. That's amazing."

"Speaking of impressed. The parade and tree lighting ceremony was probably the best I've ever been to."

"You're just saying that because you're trying to win me over."

"That's not a bad idea, but I actually mean it, so I would have said it either way. I had no idea you were capable of pulling something like that together so quickly."

"See what I mean about taking me seriously?"

Derick stopped and went wide-eyed. "You're right. I'm so sorry."

"It's okay," I said.

"No, it's not."

I didn't know what to say. It was true though. It wasn't okay and I was glad to hear him voice it.

After dinner, we opted not to get dessert, but to head on to the next event he had lined up, which I was really becoming more and more curious about. Was he going to have us get supplies to build some kind of wood project? I certainly hoped not. I was not in the mood to get all sawdusty.

Since the art studio was just a few doors down from The Pub, we opted to walk. I shoved my cold hands into my coat pocket and tilted my head down so my hair would mostly cover my cold ears.

Derick looked down at me and smiled.

"What?" I said.

"Nothing."

"C'mon. I asked you a question. You can't ignore it. You promised to take me seriously."

"It's just, I've always thought you look so cute in the cold. Your cheeks get all red and so does your nose. It's just cute, is all." He mumbled the last little bit.

"Oh," I said and quickly looked away. I had no idea what to say to that. If he didn't stop saying things like that, I would end up never talking at all.

The art store was beside the hardware store. No wonder Derick knew about it. When we walked in, I was surprised to see a group of people already inside, settled around tables that were set up like a little classroom.

"I thought this was an art store," I said, shaking the snow off of my hair.

"It is during the day. At night, it's a classroom and they

do paint nights on the weekend."

"We're going to be painting." I didn't say it as a question. It was more of a defeated statement. I was a horrible artist. Sure, I loved to design projects and plan parties, but the actual act of putting pen, pencil or even brush to paper never went very well for me.

"Yep! Fun, huh?"

I smiled and pretended to be excited. He was trying and I could at least do the same.

A lady came around and handed us each an apron, a set of brushes and some paints. I was actually a little excited to use all the tools and stuff she gave us, but it wasn't long before I realized that while painting was fun, I was just as horrible at it as I had always believed myself to be.

Derick, on the other hand, was amazing. I didn't know how I had missed his artistic side all the years I had known him. By the end of the night, I had to admit that I was actually enjoying myself. We hadn't had one single argument. He really was trying, and so was I.

By the time Derick dropped me off at my door, I was somewhat sad the night was over. It had been a really long time since I had gone out and had fun and I was worried that once that front closed for the night, we may not find our way back to this place.

"Thanks," I said at the door, trying to drag out the conversation probably longer than necessary. I'd already thanked him in the car and on the way up to the door.

"No, thank you. I had a lot of fun." His smile was bright and young. It reminded me of high school Derick.

"Oh, wait. You forgot your painting," he said and turned to run back to the car.

"Oh no, you keep that. I really don't know what I'd do with it."

"You sure? It's awesome." He paused, halfway to the car.

I laughed. "No, it is not. Did you even look at it?" I hollered back. "Jenny could have done better."

He turned back to face me and began walking toward the front porch again. "Well," he said, his voice softening as he approached the front steps. "To be fair, Jenny is really talented."

We both laughed—real laughter—and it felt so good.

"Are you sure you don't want it?" he said, meeting me at the door.

"Absolutely."

"Okay. If you say so."

There was probably about ten seconds of silence that felt like hours as we just stood there as the snow fell in soft flakes all around us. The silence seemed thickened by the snow as we waited for the other to speak, but neither apparently wanting to leave.

"Well…" He rocked back and forth on his heels.

"Well…" I countered. He wasn't going to try and kiss me, was he? I hoped not. I wasn't ready for him to try that. It sort of looked like he wanted to, and that couldn't happen. I wasn't ready to kiss him, but I also wasn't ready to turn him down.

His longing look turned into a nod and a smile and his rocking came to an abrupt halt.

"All right. Have a good night."

"You, too."

He gave me a little wave and then turned to leave as I opened the door and backed my way inside. I watched him walk to his truck. He stopped before getting in—on the driver's side this time—and turned back. I was somewhat embarrassed that he caught me watching but reminded myself I wasn't doing it to *watch him*, watch him. I was just making sure the father of my children made it to his car safely. There was nothing to be embarrassed about.

He waved one more time before starting the truck. The sight of him revving up that engine, letting it sputter a couple times before it really started made me smile. It was so like him to hang onto things for longer than they were any good.

I closed the front door and was surprised to be welcomed home by an unfamiliarly quiet house. The kids must be asleep. Just inside, I caught Lucy curled up on the couch reading a book. She wasn't even watching our tv, or eating our snacks.

I reached into my purse and pulled out my wallet. She deserved to be paid well.

"Oh," Lucy said, seeing me approach. "Mr. Winston already took care of it."

"Oh, okay." I put my wallet back. "Can I at least drive you home?"

"My mom is actually already on her way."

"Okay. Well, thank you."

"No problem. The kids were great. They went to bed at eight and have been asleep since about eight thirty. I made sure they cleaned up first and brushed their teeth."

"Amazing. Are you sure I don't owe you?" It felt wrong not to pay this angel of a teenager.

Lucy laughed. "Nah, really. Mr. Winston already sent over the money. It was more than enough."

I wondered how much he'd had to pay her to get this kind of results.

Lucy gathered her things and her mom pulled up only minutes later and she was gone.

The kids were asleep and for the first time in months I crawled into bed with no regrets or worries for the day, just gratitude.

21

DERICK

I left the house wanting so badly to stay. I knew I couldn't though, not unless she asked me. I didn't think I'd wanted to stay for anything other than feeling homesick, but I'd be lying if I said I hadn't wanted to kiss her.

I pulled up to the hardware store and as I got out of my truck, I glanced in the passenger side at that awful painting Ivy had made. It made me smile. She was typically the one who did everything right, while I was the screw up. Not that she'd screwed up the painting. I actually loved it. I loved that she'd tried something she wasn't good at.

The reason she was always so good at everything was because she only ever did things she excelled at. The painting was proof that she was trying something outside her comfort zone, and that was beautiful to me. I wished she would see it that way. I wished she would see herself the way I saw her, and not the way she thought I did.

That would have to be my goal then, over the next few days I had left. I would have to show her how I really saw her. If she could just understand how much of her I really cherished and adored, I thought she'd be happy again. I thought we'd be happy.

I walked into my studio apartment that night with her painting in hand and vowed to find a way to show her it was beautiful, that *she* was beautiful in every way. Maybe then, we could be a family.

Maybe then, I could go home.

22

IVY

I stood in my closet, glancing at the row of clothes hanging in front of me. I'd already showered, dried my hair, brushed my teeth and even managed to put some make-up on. The miracle of it all was, I didn't even have to rely on my alarm clock to get me up to get it all done.

After last night, I went to bed and must have had the best night's sleep ever because when I woke, I was alert and ready to start my day. This sort of phenomenon hadn't occurred in what felt like decades.

I finally decided on a light blue sweater and a pair of dark jeggings. It felt so nice to have time to make choices, to be able to think things through and make sure it was what I really wanted. Perhaps the answer to my biggest concerns and pleas for time to think could be resolved by just getting enough sleep.

As I leisurely sat on my bed and pulled a pair of warm socks over my chilly toes, my bedroom door was thrust open until it slammed hard against the opposite wall, a sudden and sharp contrast to the mood I had just been experiencing.

"What is going on?" I asked my nine-year-old, who stood in the doorway.

"Mom!" Her voice was frantic. "Get up!"

"I'm up. I've been up." I started to brag but stopped when I took in her tone and overall anxious demeanor.

"We don't have time! I need you to run to the store and get ink."

"Ink? At six thirty in the morning?" I chortled.

"I forgot to print my assignment last night before I went to sleep. But when I went to print it this morning, our printer wouldn't work. Today is the last day of school before break. We need ink. I can't turn it in without ink."

"Okay, calm down," I said, trying to draw back the calm I had felt just moments before. "We can't buy ink this morning. Nothing is even open until nine." The joys of living in a small town.

"Well, we're just going to have to call the store and tell them it's an emergency or something. I have to get my paper printed."

"Mal, I'm sure we can think of another way to get your assignment printed in time. I can call your teacher and…"

Mal groaned and threw her hands down at her sides. "Never mind, Mom! I'll just fail." She turned and stormed out of my room.

I refused to let this ruin my good mood. This was not the crisis she thought it was and there would be time to fix it. I stood calmly and followed her out of my room and into the hall.

"Fail? You're in the fourth grade. You can't fail."

She didn't even bother to look at me. "You wouldn't understand," she growled before descending the stairwell.

"What's going on?" a bleary-eyed Harrison asked from his bedroom doorway.

"It's nothing. Mal's just a little worked up."

"Mal's always a little worked up. Like you." Harrison yawned.

His last statement gave me pause. Was that really how my kids saw me? Worked up? No wonder Mal took everything so seriously, if that's how she saw me handle my own life. I sighed and then put my arm around Harrison, his head nearly reaching my shoulders. I bent down and kissed his forehead.

"Head downstairs. I'm making smoothies this morning," I declared.

"Cool." Harrison shook his head and his shaggy blond hair swished from side to side. I suspected he was trying to rid himself of the kiss I'd just planted there, and it made me laugh.

He turned back at the sound of my laughter and gave me a curious look but didn't say a word.

It wasn't that weird for me to laugh, was it? I shook off the look he gave me and turned toward Jenny's room where I proceeded to wake her for the day. As I knelt beside her bed and patted her back, she rolled over before slowly opening her eyes.

"Mommy?" she asked, clearly confused.

It was then, in the moment my daughter questioned my appearance in her room that I realized I had let the stress of my life get in the way of being the mom I wanted to be; *wanted*, not *had* to be. I used to love waking the kids and even making them breakfast.

Since Derick left, I had spent every night up too late working and every morning scrambling to pull things together. And now, my daughter looked at me as I woke her like I was some kind of stranger.

"Hey baby, it's time to get up." I pushed back the hair

from her eyes and rubbed her forehead with the back of my hand.

"Oh. Okay." Her voice was sweet and still a little raspy from sleep.

Coming down the steps, I saw Mal in the living room messing with the printer. "I will call your teacher and let her know I'll be bringing the paper in, Mal. You did the work. You'll get credit for it. Just relax. It doesn't need to be there first thing."

She gave me the death stare.

I chose to ignore it and walked into the kitchen to get started on the smoothies I'd promised. I threw the strawberries, bananas and yogurt into the blender and then turned on the radio to play some Christmas songs.

Glancing out the window at the fast falling snow, I decided we needed something warm to go with the smoothies. I pulled out the flour and eggs and got to work on waffles. I hadn't made waffles in ages. The Christmas music and the fat flakes of snow prompted me to pull the cinnamon down and add it to the recipe.

As I stood in my kitchen, with Mariah Carey singing Christmas ballads in the background surrounded by the smell of cinnamon and fruit, completely immersed in the Christmas spirit, I was surprised to hear a knock at the kitchen door. I looked at the clock on the stove. What would anyone be doing here at seven fifteen in the morning? My heart raced, threatening to destroy my mood.

Turning to the kitchen door behind me, my recently racing heart settled at the site of Derick through the paneled window of the door. I wasn't sure why the site of him would cause such a reaction when only days before it would have done the exact opposite, but I wasn't going to add any stress from overthinking, so instead I opened the door and let him in.

"Hey," he said, his voice still groggy.

I shivered as the cold from outside rushed in with him.

He shut the door behind him, a few flakes of snow managing to trickle in.

"Everything okay?" I asked.

He smiled and his rosy cheeks seemed to warm a bit as he held up a little box.

I squinted to get a better look. *Ink.*

"Apparently, it was a life or death situation." He shrugged.

"She called you?"

He nodded, his eyes still obviously waking up. I hadn't seen Derick's sleepy eyes in a while and forgot how cute he looked when he was tired. His soft brown eyes were a bit swollen beneath the stray wet curls that bobbed into his face. Derick stomped off the remainder of snow that clung to his boots on the mat before fully stepping into the kitchen.

"That was nice of you, but where did you find ink this early?"

"We have the same printer. I buy my ink in bulk online."

"Smart."

"Thanks." He yawned.

"Oh, good. You made it," Mal said, entering the kitchen. "I wasn't sure you'd get here in time." She reached for the ink.

"What do you say to your dad?" I asked.

"Oh, yeah. Thanks." She took the box and started opening it.

"Yeah, thanks?" I said, annoyed at her lack of sincere gratitude. "You woke him early and made him drive through the snow when the plows haven't even been out." Then I turned back to Derick.

"That was really nice of you."

"Thank you, a lot?" Mal questioned, looking between me and Derick.

"You're welcome."

The smell of cinnamon burning on the waffle iron suddenly caught my attention and I rushed back to the counter.

"You're making waffles?" Derick asked.

"Well, trying," I said, pulling the blackened square from its coffin before dumping it in the trash.

"Sorry I interrupted," Derick said, taking the blame for the burnt waffle.

"It's fine." I didn't try to take the blame back. "I can make more. You want to stay for breakfast?"

He smiled and took a couple more steps inside the kitchen.

"You can get your twenty minutes in early." I laughed at my joke.

"Oh, uh…" His smile fell and he paused. "Actually, I have somewhere I have to be."

"At seven in the morning?" I immediately regretted my attempt at a joke. Did he not want to spend his twenty minutes today?

"Yeah. It's for work."

"Oh, okay. The hardware store opens early on snowy days?" Why did I say that? It was none of my business.

"No, my other work." He laughed. "I have some chairs I need to finish before noon."

"Oh, cool. Well, thanks for saving Mal's day." I rested my hands on the counter as another attempt at a waffle sizzled in the iron beside me.

He shrugged and a small smile returned to his lips, a semblance of the one I'd stolen with my ill attempt at a joke. "No problem."

I guess I'll see you later, then?" I hadn't meant to sound so pitiful in my question.

His smile remained though. "I hope so."

And with a quick hug and kiss good morning to the kids, he was gone.

The rest of my cheery morning seemed to dull after the burnt waffle, and Derick's weird response to me asking him to stay. But I chose to remain calm and cool as the kids ate breakfast and finished getting ready. It wasn't until the older two were out the door and I'd dropped Jenny off at preschool that I let my mind wander and overthink everything Derick had said. Why hadn't he chosen to stay?

Unable to come up with any sort of explanation that wasn't an excuse, I chose to push the thought from my mind as I parked my SUV in the back of City Hall. I realized as I was walking in that I had no idea where I was supposed to meet the rest of the design team. I reached into my purse for my phone to text Angie and bumped into the back of a very tall, blond-haired man blocking the entrance.

"Oh, whoa! Sorry. I uh…Ivy?" the blond guy said in surprise.

I looked up at him, my neck craning for a minute before I realized I did know him.

"James!"

"Wow! Long time, no see." He smiled and a row of straight white teeth gleamed down at me.

"For sure. What's it been, ten years or more?" I asked.

"No. Much longer. I'm pretty certain I remember the day Ivy Gardner walked out of my life. The last time I saw you was at grad night. The night you told me you were in love with someone else."

I sighed. Ivy Gardner was not a name I'd heard in years.

"How is Derick, by the way? You guys still living in town, I assume?"

"Oh yeah, he's good. He's living above Al's Hardware and…" I trailed off. I wasn't about to explain the weird situation between Derick and I to some old high school friend.

"They're in the process of a divorce. It's tricky," I heard a voice say from behind me. I turned to find Daisy Sittoway, one hand on her hip and her snarky face giving me her usual stink eye.

What on earth was she doing at City Hall? And what gave her the right to chime in on my personal life?

"Well, we are currently separated, but I uh…" I was not prepared to discuss the finer details of my relationship with James when I wasn't even sure what they were myself.

"Oh, sorry," James said, obviously feeling awkward after Daisy's true-to-character awkward comment.

"It's fine." I paused for a second, lost as to where to take the conversation next. "What are you doing here?" I finally asked.

I saw James's shoulders relax as he shoved his hands into his pockets. "I'm actually here for work. I was just hired to work on the town Christmas Gala."

"Oh! Wow!"

"Weren't you in charge of that, Ivy?" Daisy asked, once again interrupting a conversation that she had not been invited to participate in.

"I still am, actually. The mayor had mentioned that she

would be pulling in some more people to help out. I'm so glad it's you," I said with a smile.

"Not just James," Daisy added. "It looks like all three of us will be working together. How fun!" She smiled and I swear I could see slime oozing from her soul-sucking face.

She pushed the up button on the elevator.

"Fun," I said, trying to hide my sarcasm.

Not wanting to be the only one who didn't know where the meeting was, I followed Daisy as she got on the elevator only to turn around and see James still standing outside the elevator doors.

"I'll take the stairs." He smiled mischievously and I immediately regretted following Daisy anywhere.

The meeting at City Hall went better than I had hoped, especially after having to ride that elevator alone with Daisy. The mayor's relative that worked for the previous design team was actually rather helpful. She also felt really bad for not being able to follow through with the plans for the parade and tree lighting.

I was surprised how well the two of us got along, especially considering how annoying I found the mayor. After about an hour and a half of PowerPoint presentations, catering menus and D.J. versus live band discussion, we had finalized most of the gala and were ready to get to the site to start decorating. Unfortunately, the gala location that had been decided by the previous designer, unbeknownst to me, was the Sittoway Barn. It had always made sense to hold the portion of the gala open to the entire town at a barn. It was a remake of Santa's workshop, and a barn is where the reindeer were most comfortable and easiest to care for.

Every other year, though, Santa's little workshop was separate from the gala, which I had always liked. I wouldn't have been comfortable petting reindeer and snapping photos of Santa and my kids while in jeans and a t-shirt while in full view of Holly Spring's upper class, donned in their fanciest clothes to attend the town charity event.

I despised the thought of trying to decorate Daisy's place or even working around her, but it was far too late to change the venue. It was just another level of agitation that I was not prepared for.

With Daisy's bossy face looming in my mind and only three days until the event, it felt like we were rushed but I refused to let that overwhelm me. I'd had a taste of what peace felt like last night and this morning, I was going to do all I could to keep it around a bit longer.

23

DERICK

Leaving the house that morning was one of the hardest things I've ever had to do. But I couldn't let Ivy count that visit as my twenty minutes. I had to see her in a better setting than that. I wanted it to be special.

The snow had started to slow a bit as I pulled into my shop. I couldn't hire people just yet but knew that soon it would be a reality; the first person I'd hire would be someone who could come and sort all the wood and supplies for me. It would be amazing and so much more efficient once I had this place organized. But for now, it worked and would have to until I at least finished my current project. It was a pretty big one.

The Sittoways had hired me to install cabinets in both of their kitchens. They were so wealthy, they had two kitchens. From what I could tell, neither one of them were used all that often, but who was I to argue with such a big paycheck? I was loading up my truck with the last bit of supplies to take back to the Sittoways with me when I had an idea. I thought about the painting Ivy had made and how beautiful it was to me. I was sure I could find time before Christmas to make a frame for it. Of course, it couldn't be her entire present, but it was possibly a good start.

I closed the hatch to the truck, the wood barely fitting inside. Perhaps it wouldn't be long before I needed to buy a bigger loading truck as well. I trudged through the snow and climbed in.

I shivered and wished I had thought to bring a hat, or even a better coat. It was certainly getting a bit cold in the cab, with that passenger side window always stuck open. But I was loyal and would drive this baby as long as she'd let me. She'd been a great truck and the little hiccups were no reason for me to throw her out.

I turned the key in the ignition, listening as it sputtered and then stopped. I tried again three more times with the same result. "No," I whispered. "Not today. Please." I said a small prayer, hoping it would bring the miracle I needed. In it, I asked for just another day at least, so I could get through this project and get paid. I almost felt guilty for only asking for one day, like I didn't believe in the truck or something.

I tried it one more time. The engine stuttered and spit and finally roared to life. I hooted and hollered as I peeled away from the warehouse and headed into town. I would have spun a couple of donuts if I didn't have a truck load full of lumber.

As I pulled into the Sittoway's Ranch, I was surprised to see Ivy's SUV parked in front of the barn. Why would Ivy be at the Sittoway's? For all I knew, she couldn't stand Daisy. Out of complete curiosity, I took the long way to the house and drove past the barn to get a better look. It was definitely Ivy's car, but there was no Ivy in sight. I didn't have time or a real excuse that would warrant me going into the barn, so I decided I'd pry the info out of Ivy, or possibly Daisy, as soon as I was given the chance.

24

IVY

*O*nce inside the Sittoway's barn, I had to admit it was a great place to throw the Christmas Gala, but I kept that in my head. I could not give a compliment to someone so full of herself already; it wouldn't be fair to any of us.

"Where do you want us, boss?" James asked, sneaking up behind me.

I laughed. "Please, you do not need to call me boss."

"What would you prefer I call you? I can think of plenty of other nicknames from high school, if you'd like."

"No, that's all right. I'm sure those would not be work appropriate."

"Probably not, but I'm sure at least one of them is still accurate."

I turned around to face James, unable to refrain from catching his bait. "And what nickname might that be?"

James laughed. "You already said it wouldn't be appropriate for work."

I rolled my eyes. "Fine. We should get started with the lights anyway."

"Sounds good," Daisy said, coming to stand beside me

and James. "I had some brought up already that I thought would go well with the rustic look the barn already has."

Of course she did. I wondered how much of this she had already planned on her own and how much of it I would have to work around in order to keep our venue.

"Sure. We can take a look and see what might work with the plans we already have in place," I said, doing my best to sound professional.

Her eyebrows rose in annoyance before she turned on her heels and walked away.

I looked back at James who was suppressing a laugh. "Well, she hasn't changed much, has she?"

I clicked my tongue. "Not at all."

"I suppose her high school nickname still works too."

I gave James an inquisitive look.

"Hot head," he whispered, and I laughed. It was nice to have a friend at work that wasn't preoccupied with making a name for themselves.

Daisy returned with two men I'd never met before, each carrying a giant box of lights.

"You can put them here," she said, pointing at my feet.

"Oh! Cool. Thanks," I said, trying to sound more grateful than I was. It wasn't their fault she was insane.

"I don't think these lights are going to work," James said, shaking his head as he gave them a once over. I could tell he was just saying it to get on my good side. The lights were fine, actually pretty similar to the ones we had decided to purchase and use.

Daisy sighed and her usual strong, annoying demeanor seemed to fall some.

We really didn't have time to be petty, I reminded myself. "I don't know. They're already here, and they're about the right size."

Daisy's face lit up.

"Why don't we give them a try. We could start in the far corner, where the photo booth will be. If we don't like how they look over there, we can always switch to the other ones we discussed earlier.

"Okay!" Daisy said with a smile before bullying her two spare men into carrying the boxes to the other end of the barn for her. I hadn't thought about them having to move them all.

As Daisy and her cabana boys walked away with the lights, James leaned down and whispered in my ear. "I guess we'll have to change that nickname a little to fit the new, more accommodating you."

"I don't know what you're talking about," I said.

The rest of the afternoon was spent hanging lights and setting up tables and chairs. If we could get all the bones of the gala put together that day, we'd have time to complete the rest in the following three days. Thanks to the help of my mom and Derick, the kids were pretty much taken care of and I was able to get through the project in time for the food, music and visitors to arrive the night of the gala.

25

DERICK

Ivy worked nonstop for the three days leading up to the gala. It did not make my plans to woo her back into my arms any easier. Thankfully, I had finished up at the Sittoway's house and was able to watch the kids, and made the most of the pickups and drop-offs with Ivy.

The day before the gala, I even surprised her with her favorite lunch from The Pub. She seemed relieved for the break and when our twenty minutes was up, she actually asked if I wanted to stick around a bit longer to try some of the desserts they'd gotten for the event. The desserts were awesome and while Ivy was mostly busy decorating and instructing, it was nice to be near her. With only four days until our twelve days were scheduled to end, I really thought things were going well. I had mostly convinced myself the divorce papers may find their way to a trash can, after all. I may not have made enough progress yet to secure an end to our separation, but I felt confident that the divorce was no longer looming in the not-so-distant future.

That night, I stopped by the house to let the kids get an extra pair of clothes since they were going to be spending a little bit longer than planned at my place. While they raced up the stairs to grab what they needed, Ivy invited me to sit in the front room.

It was the first time I'd noticed how empty the room looked, at least for the season.

"Where's the Christmas tree?" I asked, mostly expecting that she had decided to move it somewhere else this year. It was always her favorite part of the holiday.

"I didn't get around to putting it up this year," she said in defeat.

"What? No way. But you love decorating. It's like your favorite part of the holiday."

"I guess I've been too busy decorating for everyone else. It's too late now. Christmas is in three days."

"It's not too late."

"C'mon, Derick. Where would I even find a tree this late?"

"So, if you had a tree, you'd decorate it?"

"Well...I guess. But it seems like a pointless venture this late in the game."

I thought for a second, and then remembered the pines that surrounded my shop. They might be huge, but...

"What are your plans tonight?" I asked, not thinking about how forward it sounded. I'd already soaked up our twenty minutes for the day.

"Uh... I was actually just going to sit and watch Christmas movies and get some takeout. I didn't really have anything for tonight."

I glanced at my watch. It was only four o'clock. "Could you watch the kids for a while? I forgot something."

She looked at me with confusion and, if I was reading her right, a little disappointment in her eyes.

"Yeah," she finally said.

I laughed a little. "There's just something I wanted to pick up. Maybe I could grab the take-out too? Do you want to call it in, and I can grab it for you? My treat," I added.

Her face seemed to relax. "Uh, sure."

"Give me about an hour and a half before you call in the food. I'll run my errand and then be back with dinner."

I didn't bother even telling the kids bye. I got up and left as quickly as I could. When I got to the truck, I realized, while I could probably fit the tree in the back, I would need at least another set of hands to help. That's when I remembered Oliver. He was always available when I needed someone. He'd fixed my truck's door in an afternoon and was far more capable than just that. Not only was he the local handyman, he ran the only salvage yard in town. I was certain he wouldn't just be willing to help, he also may have some tools to get the job done quicker.

I pulled my phone out and dialed Oliver's number.

Oliver met me at the shop. I had never been more grateful to see the lumberjack of a man in my life. I pulled him in for a quick hug and thanked him for responding to my call for help on such short notice.

His truck may have been as old as mine, but it definitely looked to be in much better shape. He offered to load the tree in it, since mine was mostly full of lumber. I gratefully agreed. He pulled out his toolbox from the cab, along with a giant chainsaw.

I couldn't express the amount of gratitude I felt when I realized how truly impossible this project would have been on my own. Thankfully, with Oliver, it was just a matter of following his lead and helping him lug the giant spruce into that back of his truck.

"You want me to follow you back?" he asked.

"That would be perfect. I just need to swing by The Pub on my way home."

It was the first time in months that I had accidentally called Ivy's place home, but I didn't bother correcting myself. I just hoped the slip was a sign of good things to come. Before pulling away from the shop, I called The Pub and added a burger and fries to the order Ivy had already placed. It was the least I could do to say thanks to Oliver. Heaven knew, I owed him much more.

By the time we got back to Ivy's, it was nearly seven. I hoped I wasn't too late for dinner and that she wouldn't be angry. I really wanted this to go well.

Before unloading the tree, I ran up to the door and knocked. Ivy answered, her face a mixture of confusion and excitement. What's Oliver Oliverard doing here?" she asked, spotting his truck in the driveway.

"I couldn't carry it by myself."

"Carry what?"

I just laughed and motioned for her to walk out to his truck with me. Her cheeks were

already tinged with pink before she left the house; I couldn't tell if it was from nerves or the onslaught of cool air.

"A tree!" She hit my arm.

I just smiled.

"Thank you." She looked at me, sincerity wetting her eyes.

"Of course," I said, "but really Oliver was the one who did the real work." I gave Oliver a thumbs up to let him know we were good to unload it here. I'd told him it was a surprise and he insisted we make sure it was okay with her before we brought it into the house. He gave me a nod and a smile before getting out into the snow to finish the project we'd started.

While the kids devoured the takeout, Oliver and I got the tree inside and set up in the front window. I was amazed and relieved at how well it fit.

"Thanks, again, man." I patted Oliver on the back.

"Glad I could help," he said.

I gave him his takeout. He looked in the bag and he laughed. "You know me too well."

I must have gotten him something he liked. I was honestly just guessing.

"I hope it's not cold."

"I'm sure it will be fine," he said as he exited the house and walked back toward his truck.

"Have a good night," he called as he reached into his takeout bag to pull out a handful of fries.

"Will do," I responded before I turned back to the house that held my future.

26

IVY

The kids finished their dinner while Derick and Oliver put the tree up and I gathered all the ornaments from the attic—the ornaments I thought we'd leave until at least next year. But seeing the tree in the front room and smelling that fresh pine smell made everything else finally feel like Christmas.

I watched Oliver walk Derick out to his truck and felt a sudden surge of gratitude for Derick. Not only did he come through for us, he did it in a way I hadn't expected. Honestly, he'd done a lot for us recently, a lot for me.

He stood in the cold without his coat on, his flannel shirt hanging over his jeans that were now covered in pine needles. He waved and hollered out thanks as Oliver pulled out of the driveway. It was almost as if he still lived here, as if he never left, and I suddenly wished it to be true.

The thought caught me off guard. Did I really want Derick to move back home?

The door opened and Derick shook the snow off of his broad shoulders before entering. I remained at the front room window, afraid he would read my expression and know how much this meant to me or that he'd be able to see how badly I wanted him to come home.

The kids were still eating in the kitchen and the front room felt very secluded as Derick stepped inside it, a warm smile on his lips. Out of the corner of my eyes, I saw him rub his hands together. He was cold and my first instinct was to remedy that.

I turned with my arms folded, not thinking about what my face might reveal and asked if he wanted me to turn the fireplace on.

"That would be great." He chuckled.

"You're probably hungry, too. Sit down. I'll bring your food in."

"Are you sure?"

I usually complained whenever anyone tried to eat in the front room. But I was done

being worked up. I nodded with a simple, "Yeah," before turning the switch on the electric fireplace and leaving to grab our food that I'd left on the kitchen counter.

With brown bags weighed down by grease, I reached for a stack of paper towels before heading back into the front room. Derick sat on the loveseat nearest the fireplace, warming his hands.

I opted to sit on the floor in front of the fireplace instead of beside him on the loveseat. I wasn't sure what being in such close proximity would do to my already appreciative mood and I was trying to be careful.

I laid out a couple rolls of paper towels before pulling out the burgers and fries. I breathed in the smell. I was such a burger and onion rings girl. The Pub had the best onion rings. All those fancy meals and recipes were completely lost on me.

Derick must have caught me, cuz he chuckled.

I looked up at him and couldn't help but smile back.

"Thanks," he said, shifting from the loveseat to join me on the floor. I hadn't expected him to do that. I felt his arm brush against mine and goosebumps rushed up to my shoulders and down my neck.

I hadn't expected that either.

I waited for him to unwrap his burger before taking my first bite. It probably wasn't as hot as it had been when it first got here but it was still delicious.

"Thank you," I finally said around a mouth full of onion rings. "The tree looks amazing."

"No problem," he said, before biting into his burger. We were both starving, and it felt so comfortable to sit here and relax beside the tree and eat.

I finished my onion rings first and he offered me the last of his. My hand brushed against his in my rush to accept them and we both paused for the smallest of seconds before resuming our ravenous eating.

The kids joined us before we had finished our meal and were jumping up and down with excitement about how they were going to decorate the tree, who would string the lights and who would place the star.

They became silent before I realized they were waiting on me to tell them what to do. I typically was pretty uptight about how the tree looked. I always went in with a game plan and then directed the kids like little minions to complete my vision. I looked at their expectant faces and just laughed.

"Have at it!" I said.

"What?" Mal's face was contorted in confusion.

"Go for it. Dad and I will join in when we finish eating."

"Okay…" Mal said, her voice still apprehensive as she reached for the box labeled *lights*. I didn't say a word. I did, however, catch a glimpse of Derick's surprised face from the corner of my eye and wanted to laugh at how good it felt to not only surprise them all, but to let things go just a bit.

Mal and Harrison worked to hang the lights together. It was a tad awkward looking and didn't quite reach the top of the tree, but I was determined to keep my mouth shut.

Jenny had her hands in the box of ornaments and tinsel before the lights were even up and had created a very cluttered corner near her eye level, her version of Christmas magic.

Wiping the grease on my hands onto a paper towel, I pulled my phone from my pocket and searched for my music app before hitting play on my Christmas songs list.

With Dean Martin and Frank Sinatra serenading us, Derick and I joined in until the last of the box of ornaments was empty.

"It looks great, guys!" Derick said, eyeing our cluttered and non-themed tree. I smiled and had to agree. It was the best tree I think our family had ever had in our home.

27

DERICK

I offered to take the kids home for the night as we had planned, but with Jenny crashed beneath the tree like an exhausted little sugar plum in her purple and pink tutu, Ivy said they'd be fine to stay the night. She didn't need to be at the barn until ten, and I offered to pick the kids up by eight. The older two had shuffled upstairs to brush and get ready for bed, leaving Ivy and I alone to say goodnight.

"I had a really fun time tonight," I said.

"Me too," she admitted, and it felt honest. "Thank you again for the tree and…" Her words trailed off.

What else was she thanking me for? I wish I knew what she was thinking.

"It was my pleasure," I said, taking a step toward the door. "I'll be back in the morning for the kids. If you need me earlier, just call." I reached for the doorknob when I remembered my coat. I turned around to grab it only to discover that Ivy had been walking me to the door and was now inches from my face.

"Oh!" she said, but she didn't seem upset. Just surprised. We stood there, inches from each other. I could smell her perfume, the same lilac and vanilla smell she always wore. I wanted nothing more than to wrap that smell and her along with it up in my arms and never let go.

"Kiss her!!" Mal and Harrison called from the steps.

Ivy laughed as she took a step back and her eyes glanced above me.

My eyes followed hers to the mistletoe that hung from the doorway.

Who put that there? I was about to ask but didn't want to destroy any chance there might be of this actually working.

"C'mon, kiss her!" Mal repeated.

Ivy laughed and let her gaze fall back to mine. I looked down into her eyes, her beautifully bright green eyes, before my gaze traveled down to her soft, pink lips, slightly parted in a smile.

I took that smile as my sign and went for it, leaning in slightly. I was relieved when her lips met mine without resistance. Her hands traveled up my chest to wrap around the back of my neck as my hands instinctively slid around her waist.

Her lips were soft against mine and I found it hard to let her go, but then her lips went still. I was not going to push her to do something she wasn't ready for. I let my hands go limp before they fell to my sides and she slipped hers from around my neck.

"The power of mistletoe," she whispered, before looking back at the kids.

They cheered before she shushed and then pointed to the still-sleeping Jenny.

"Get up in bed," she reprimanded. "Your dad will be back early in the morning to pick you up."

With the kids out of sight, she turned back to me. I was silent, stoic, afraid to move for fear of ruining the moment.

"Well," she said, rubbing her hands over her arms.

After a moment of silence, I contemplated pulling her back in my arms and kissing her all over again, only this time it would be a real kiss and not one in front of the kids. Instead, I cleared my throat.

"Do you want me to lay Jenny in her bed for you?"

"Nah, I can take her."

I wanted to argue, anything to stay longer, but I also knew she didn't like me to push my help on her.

"I guess I'll see you in the morning, then."

"Right." She reached for my coat on the coat rack. "Don't forget this."

"Thanks." I took the coat and felt her hand graze mine. I clutched the coat tightly to keep myself from being more forward than she was ready for.

"Good night," she said as I backed up to the door.

"Night." I turned the knob and exited back into the cold night air.

28

IVY

I lay in bed wide-eyed as I replayed the evening's events in my mind. I wanted so badly to call Derick up on the phone right then and there and tell him to come back. I needed him back. I wanted him back in my life.

I put my fingertips to my lips, remembering the way his mouth felt around mine. It was a quick kiss, but it was full of so much emotion and passion that it left me stupid. Literally stupid. I should have spoken up before he left. I knew the moment his lips touched mine that I had been missing him. I knew exactly what I wanted at that moment, but I let it slip by and didn't say a word.

Before I drifted off to sleep, I promised myself that I would tell him how I felt, regardless of how much I wanted him to say it first. This time, I was not going to wait for him to come back and say he needed me. I was going to speak up and say what I really wanted.

DERICK

The morning of the gala, I woke early to pick up the kids from the house. If last night wasn't an indication of good things to come, I didn't know what was. After the kiss, I had wanted nothing more than to stay and be a family again, but I also wanted to make sure Ivy was ready and that she really knew how much she meant to me.

I grabbed my keys and my coat as I headed out of the loft, hopefully for one of the last times ever, and down to my truck. It must have snowed all night, because the truck was covered. It took me nearly twenty minutes to clear it off before I was able to crawl in.

I turned the key in the ignition but heard nothing, not even a sputter or hiccup. It just sat there. Of course, of all the times not to run, it had to be today when Ivy was counting on me to pick up the kids.

I tried again, but nothing.

I hung my head in defeat. I could walk to the house and pick the kids up, but then they would have to trek in the snow back to my place. I couldn't imagine that going well.

I could call someone to give me a ride. I pulled out my

phone and looked through my list of contacts, but none of the names stuck out as someone I could call this early in the morning without being a total bother. I wished so badly that I still had family in town. My dad would have helped in a heartbeat. Unfortunately, living over twelve hundred miles away in sunny Hawaii was not a heartbeat away at all, not to mention the time difference. Even calling them just to chat would be cruel.

The closest thing I had to family in the area was Ivy and the kids, and well, I guessed I could count Marjorie. She was technically family. My thumb paused on her number in my phone. Could I? Did I dare?

She would totally help, if only to make me look bad.

Whether good or bad, I decided in that moment what mattered most was making sure Ivy made it to the venue in time to get her job done. I clicked on Marjorie's name and the number dialed quickly. A little too quickly. I hardly had time to think through what I would say before my mother-in-law's shrill voice came on the other end.

"Hello, Derick," she said.

"Marjorie?" I asked for some reason, partially hoping I'd dialed wrong and could go back and rethink my game plan.

"Is everything okay with Ivy and the kids?" she asked, worry evident in her voice.

I truly never called the woman. Of course she went to the worst case scenario first.

"Yes, yes. Everyone is fine."

"Oh, thank heavens." There was a long pause where I debated telling her I had butt dialed her. She waited, her breathing sounding annoyed as she waited for me to speak.

"I'm sorry to call so early."

"It may be early for you, dear, but I get up with the crow."

She meant it to be kind, but it felt like she was mocking me for thinking seven thirty was early.

"Right. Of course. We, that is…I mean, Ivy has a big day today and I had planned to take the kids, but my truck won't start. I wasn't sure who else to call. I didn't want—"

"Why didn't Ivy ask me to begin with? She knows I'm reliable."

I held in the sigh that would potentially annoy her more.

"What time am I needed?"

"Oh, thank you, Marjorie. If you could just pick me up, I'll take care of the kids today. I just need a ride."

"I would be happy to watch my grandchildren, Derick. I don't think it's necessary for you to be involved at this point. I'm free and Ivy needs help."

I knew I shouldn't have called her.

"I can take care of my kids," I repeated. "I just need a lift to get there."

"You obviously called me for help, Derick. Please don't negotiate how I offer it."

She always had a way of making me feel like an idiot—an ill-mannered idiot. I didn't say anything as we sat, once again, through another awkward silence. I glanced at the present for Ivy on my passenger seat. She deserved to get to work on time, regardless of how it made me look.

"Thank you for your help. She needs to leave by nine."

"Very well. I will make sure I am there by eight forty, sharp."

"Thank you, Marjorie."

"Well then. Best of luck with your, uh, truck." She hung up. Not so much as a goodbye or anything. I got out of my cold truck and trudged up the snowy walk to the back of the hardware store. I was doing exactly what Ivy said I always did on a day that she really needed me. Just when I thought we actually stood a chance. I dreaded the next phone call I had to make and probably put it off too long.

By the time I got the courage to call Ivy and let her know that I wasn't going to be able to pick up the kids, her mother had already intervened and told her version of the story.

"It's fine, Derick," Ivy insisted, but I could tell she was disappointed. She had put her faith in me, and I had failed again.

"I'll get someone to come look at the truck as soon as I can and then maybe I can swing by and get the kids from your mom."

"It's fine, really. She seemed happy to have a day with them and they don't seem to mind."

I wanted to ask to see her later but felt like it was a bad time to bring it up, on the heels of my failure. I couldn't imagine she would want much to do with me and I was feeling pretty sorry for myself.

"Oh shoot, she's here. I gotta go." She sounded stressed.

In the background, I could hear Marjorie's voice. She must have just let herself in. I hated when she would do that.

"Okay. I'll talk to you later," I said, my voice a little too pathetic for my own good.

"Hey mom, thanks for showing up on such short notice…" Ivy's voice trailed off as her attention was drawn away. I disconnected the line and set the phone down on my kitchen table, letting my head follow suit as the cool countertop connected with my forehead.

I had two days left in my plan to convince my wife that I was not a total screw up, that I could follow through and be there for her; two days to get her to fall back in love with me and I was stuck in my apartment letting someone else help when it should have been me. When she had counted on it being me.

After a thirty-minute pity party, I decided I still had time and I was not going to throw in the towel and do nothing. I needed to win my wife back and that was exactly what I was going to do. Sure, my mother-in-law came in and stole my heroic plan out from under me, but I could still show Ivy that I cared and adored her. I could still show up and be there.

By 10:00 a.m., I had a plan in place and was surprisingly grateful for my mother-in-law's interference. Her taking the kids actually freed me up to surprise Ivy and hopefully win her back before the two days were up.

I pulled out my phone again, said a quick prayer, and made a couple of calls. With God's grace, she'd be back in my arms tonight and those crummy divorce papers would be at the bottom of a trash can where they belonged.

The first call was to Al. He and I were about the same size and I knew from years of working for him that he owned a tux. I was pretty sure he'd only worn it once to his brother's wedding, and it was probably dusty, but it was better than anything I had and I needed to look like a gala attendee and not like the rest of the townspeople who stopped by to view the lights and barn animals before the gala would begin.

The last thing I needed was someone to help with the truck. I'd called around all afternoon but couldn't find a single car place open or willing to make house calls. That left Joey, the fry cook at The Bell, but also a brilliant car guy. We didn't know each other too well, but I had heard great things about how quick he was with car repairs and I needed a mechanic fast.

Thankfully, The Bell was closed down for some kind of baking event and Joey wasn't needed behind the grill for breakfast that day. Once I promised to pay in cash, he dropped whatever he was doing and met me at my truck.

He diagnosed the problem in minutes. The alternator was

going out. The cold weather wasn't helping. Unfortunately, he didn't have a replacement part for my particular truck on hand. He'd have to order it and it probably wouldn't arrive until after Christmas.

"Isn't there anything you can do? I sort of need it to work, even if it's just for tonight."

"I can charge the battery and jump it for you. It'll start up, but I can't promise that it will start again after you've turned it off."

"That's okay." If everything went as planned, I'd happily walk home.

Joey agreed to jump it and by five, my truck was up and running. Per Joey's instructions, I did not turn it off for fear that it would not start again. I left it idling on the street while I ran back inside to get the present for Ivy and quickly change into the tux Al had brought by. I took a minute to glance in the mirror and brushed my hair back with my hands, then leaned forward to check the progress of my facial hair. Noting the clock and my lack of time, I decided what I had was going to have to do.

30

IVY

Standing in the center of the once plain and empty barn, I motioned for the crew to hit the lights. The flood lights switched off and for the briefest moment, I was surrounded in pitch black. Slowly and almost magically, the white Christmas lights flickered into view, illuminating the entire barn in a soft white glow emphasizing the classical details of the decor. The rafters housed white linens that swooped between them until they glided gracefully down the walls.

Sixty-four tables circled the room, each of them shrouded in their own small ceramic Christmas scenes, with flakes of fake snow scattered across the top.

I turned toward the middle of the room. The dance floor was clear and beautiful. Placing the shiny wooden floor over top of the barn floor had been my biggest worry. I hadn't wanted to detract from the overall rustic feel of it venue, but dancing would be much safer on a clean surface. In the end, as I stared out over the entire scene, I knew we'd made the right choice. A few scattered spotlights shone randomly as the band set up and tuned their instruments. Thirty more minutes, and the guests would begin to arrive; I couldn't be happier with how it all had turned out.

The Christmas gala had always been my favorite town tradition and while it was a lot of work to pull together, I was giddy with nostalgic joy to have participated on the level that I did.

Most years, we'd only stopped in to see the reindeer or meet Santa outside the gala. Tickets to get in and be seated were always on the pricier side and didn't really allow for families to come. But it always went to a good cause and I was grateful that this year, the town had decided to fund the Volunteer Firemen Foundation. Not only did it mean that the brave volunteers would be getting much needed funding, but it also meant that many of them, who couldn't typically afford to attend such an affair, would be our honored guests.

As I walked toward their designated table, I felt a tap on my shoulder. I turned abruptly and was immediately met with a giant barreled chest. I had to glance up to get the full scope of James.

"Oh, hey!" I said.

"It looks beautiful, Ivy. You've always had that ability, though."

"What?" I asked, confused. "What ability?"

"To make everything around you beautiful. I think that must be—"

My walkie buzzed. "Ivy?" A woman's voice interrupted James, which I was glad for. He had been acting super clingy the last couple of days. Sure, we were high school friends, but I didn't need to relive the good old days as much as he clearly wanted to.

I put my finger up in front of James. "Just a sec. Sorry." I motioned to my watch to remind him we were less than thirty minutes from guests arriving. I really and truly did not have time to walk down memory lane.

He nodded and smiled, but as I walked away, I could have sworn he followed me.

"What's going on?" I asked into my walkie.

"It's the reindeer. Prancer is uh, he might have gotten into something he shouldn't have."

"Where are you?" I asked, panic rising in my voice.

"Just outside the barn. We've already got a line of kids waiting to see Santa and I..." The

Walkie went to static. By the time I got to the side of the barn that was set up for the North Pole scene, Prancer had gotten loose and was braying and bucking near the line of kids. I rushed to stop him before he hurt someone. I wasn't exactly sure what I had intended to do, but I needed to calm him down.

Fortunately, just before I reached him, a hand gripped my shoulder. It was James. "Stay back. He'll hurt you." He stepping in front of me and wrapped one of his huge hands around Prancer's collar. He placed his other hand on the deer's back and started patting it, coaxing it to follow him to a less crowded area. I followed too. Perhaps, in my haste to get the animal away from all the guests, I'd followed a little too closely because as James neared the opposite end of the barn, near Prancer's gated area, she reared back, bumping into me hard and subsequently sending me to the ground.

It was then, that a group of stable hands showed up and took over, corralling the deer back inside her pen.

I sat on the wet ground, hay and mud mixed with freshly fallen snow saturating into the back my nicest dress. Nothing seemed hurt physically, but I felt like an idiot and probably looked awful. My one and only fancy dress, was most certainly smudged with mud all down my backside. Why was my only nice dress white?

James knelt at my side.

"Are you okay?" he questioned; his voice full of concern.

"I think I'm fine," I said, trying to pull myself up to my knees.

"No, don't move. Let me."

Before I could say a word, he had scooped me into his arms and was carrying me. None of it was at all necessary. My cheeks began to flush as he paraded me passed guests to who-knows-where.

"I'm really fine," I half said, half groaned. My groaning was out of annoyance but I soon

regretted it as he must have taken it as a sign of pain.

"Shhh. Don't speak." He held his fingers to my lips and I wanted to scream from the excess of attention and lack of real listening. Finally, he set me down. My butt sat on something crunchy. I glanced down to see a pile of hay. He'd set my muddy butt on a pile of hay. Now I would really look like I had just come from the pig sty.

"I'm really fine," I said as he knelt in front of me, his face inches from mine.

"Let me just get a good look at you." He placed one hand on my bare knee and the other on the back of my head. "Don't move," he instructed. "I'm checking for a concussion."

As I was about to tell him to back the heck up and give me my space, I heard a familiar voice from somewhere behind the oaf that was James.

"What's going on here?" Derick asked in a less than amused or even concerned tone. He sounded angry.

"I'm—" I started to say but James cut me off.

"Ms. Gardner is fine. I've got it under control."

I looked at James, confused by the use of my maiden name.

"I'm sure you do," Derick responded.

I shoved James to the side as best as an ant might shove a giant. But he barely budged enough for me to see Derick turn and walk away.

"Wait, Derick!" I hollered but he didn't respond.

I could only imagine what he thought he saw.

"Stop moving, Ives!" James reprimanded, using Derick's nickname for me.

"No! You stop!" I finally said in anger. "And all you can call me is Mrs. Winston."

That seemed to get his attention.

"You're getting divorced. Why keep his—?"

"No, I'm not getting a divorce. And I'm fine. Back up! I don't need you breathing in my face or fawning all over me. I didn't hit my head or break any bones. I fell on my butt in the mud and you are too close."

James paused and looked at me like I was some kind of idiot or possibly as if I really were concussed and not making sense.

I looked down and grabbed his clammy hand that he'd planted on my knee and much of my thigh and pushed it off.

"I…uh…" he stuttered. "I thought you were hurt, and I thought—"

"You thought you could touch me and carry me and cross all kinds of boundaries without asking me even once."

"I thought you were into me," he said, surprised.

"Into you? I'm married!"

"Separated," he corrected.

I sighed and stood from the bale of hay he'd set me on.

"Next time you think you're being some knight in shining armor, please, if your supposed damsel is able to speak, ask if she wants your help."

I stood firmly on my feet before storming off to find Derick. I had some explaining to do.

31

DERICK

I couldn't believe I had read things so wrong. I really thought I had won her back. But the proof was evident in the man's arms that held her. I was the furthest thing from her mind.

Frustrated and only thinking of the shortest way to get out of there, I trudged my snowy boots through the middle of the gala and stomped past arriving guests. I squeezed my way through the entrance, making it appear much more dramatic than I had intended.

Once back outside, I trudged through the snow toward my truck, which I had, on the exact opposite recommendation of my mechanic, turned off. I stood outside the truck and kicked the tires. Why had I not just bought a new truck months ago? I could have afforded one. I always hung onto things far longer than necessary.

Maybe that was what I had done with Ivy, too. I didn't bother to try and start the dumb truck. Instead, I decided to hoof it back to town, back to my empty, lonely loft to spend Christmas Eve alone.

I pulled the collar of my coat up around my neck, wishing

I'd just let my beard grow. The Sittoway's barn was only a mile or so from the back end of town. I figured if I kept walking, I'd get to the back of City Hall in less than twenty minutes. And City Hall was only a block or so away from the hardware store.

I kept walking, replaying the events of the last two weeks in my mind as I did. How had I been so wrong about Ivy? Had I imagined the moments we shared? Did I make them out to be more than they really were? What about the night before? We'd *kissed*.

I felt a snowflake land on my nose. Angrily, I swatted it away. Of course it would snow now and ruin Al's stupid tux. Of course I was in a tux, cold and pathetic and alone. I couldn't believe I had thought twelve days was enough time to recover a marriage that had been failing for years. Ivy was right. Love wasn't enough. She'd said it. I should have respected her decision and moved on.

The snow picked up and soon, all I could see in front of me were blurs of white. I did my best to keep walking straight, hoping the direction I'd picked to go in the first place was truly leading me back into town.

Seconds before I decided I was well and truly lost and should turn back for the barn, I caught sight of lights in the distance—tiny sparkling lights. I thought I heard the roar of an engine but didn't bother to look behind me. Even if I did, I probably wouldn't see the source behind the noise in all this snow. With my hands shoved in my pockets and my head cast downward, I heard my name through the blanket of snow.

"Derick," the voice called.

It sounded like Ivy.

I didn't turn. I was probably imagining things.

"Derick." The voice came again, followed by the sound of a car door shutting.

I stopped walking and looked up. I'd made it to City Hall, or more accurately a little to the left, but was about twenty feet away from the town Christmas tree that stood in front of it.

"Derick, stop." I turned, not sure what to expect, not even hoping it was her.

She walked toward me, her white gown practically blending in with her surroundings. But her eyes—her beautiful green eyes—stood out and pled with me to come to her more than any other light could.

I took a step in her direction and then froze. It was the first time in the last two weeks I didn't have words spilling out of my mouth. I was legitimately speechless.

She walked toward me until she was just inches from my reach. I kept my hands at my sides, afraid of how they might betray me.

Her blonde hair had been pulled up into some sort of knot on top of her head and pieces spilled out and onto her face, growing damp as the snow fell. Her cheeks were rosy beneath her concerned green eyes. Only missing her halo, I saw her as an angel.

"Derick." She was out of breath and when she seemed to realize I was staying put, she took a minute to slow down, exhaling before letting the cool air back into her nostrils. I'm not sure how long we both stood there and looked at each other, freezing in the cold, but it simultaneously felt like only seconds had passed and like an eternity.

She reached her hand out and placed it on my forearm.

"I don't know what you think was happening back there," she began, "but it was not what it looked like. I fell into the mud and that idiot James thought he was helping me or something. I—"

Helping himself was more like it, I wanted to say, but the words remained in my head.

"Look, I was so angry at you before, for leaving. I hated you for a long time because you left."

"And I left tonight, again." How many times was I going to walk out?

She sighed. "No, I mean yes you did, but that was understandable. I mean, when we separated. You left that night and I wanted you to fight for us. I never wanted you to leave, but you did and then I just grew angrier and more resentful. But last night, the last eleven days really, you have done nothing but fight for us. And after…"

My anger, that had slowly been cooling since I'd left the barn had fizzled to nothing but concern and apprehension at her next words.

"After we kissed?" I finished her sentence, unable to wait any longer to hear her feelings aloud.

"Yes." She shivered and it dawned on me that she didn't have a coat. She had been standing there in the snow in nothing more than a sleeveless ball gown. I slid out of Al's tux jacket and put it over her shoulders.

She smiled. "Thank you."

"You were saying?" I prompted.

"Right. Last night, I realized I didn't fight for us either. I was the one who asked you to leave. I was the one who brought up the divorce. I was mad at you for not coming back, for not fighting for us, but I did the same thing, if not worse. I never should have given up. I'm so sorry. I—"

I didn't let her finish. I slipped one arm around her waist and cupped my other hand behind her head and pulled her toward me until there was nothing between us. I was done waiting. Her soft lips connected with mine and I released all the emotions I had been feeling since that moment in the kitchen when I realized I could lose her for good.

I held her, our bodies intertwined so completely that I wasn't sure where she began and I ended. I kissed her like I had wanted to since last night, like I should have every day for the last sixteen years.

EPILOGUE

IVY

Derick and I stood beside the town Christmas tree, its lights the perfect backdrop to our otherwise white-out of an evening. I shivered at his side but didn't want to let the perfection of the moment slip away too quickly.

With his arm around my shoulder and my head nestled against his chest, we stood and looked over the tree. I searched for our ornament, and found it quickly, remembering the awful night when I had thought he'd kissed Daisy Sittoway and given up on us. I marveled at the change that could happen in just twelve days when two people truly tried.

Derick must have been thinking something similar because he leaned down and whispered in my ear, "I promise I will always fight for you."

I smiled as his breath tickled my ear and his vow warmed my heart.

I reached out for our ornament. "You should have been with us when we placed this the first time," I said. "Let's never do that again."

"Never."

Big flakes of snow dropped from the sky, and seemed to

hover all around us, as if time stood still, and nothing in the world mattered beyond that moment. I held the ornament in my hand and Derick placed his strong hand over mine. The two of us placed it back on the tree, together as we always should have, as I knew we always would.

I backed away from the tree and caught sight of the hourglass ornament that hung just above our little family emblem. I leaned back in to get a better look, to see the strange sand flow as if its time was endless. As I cradled the ornament in my hand, I was surprised and a little disappointed to see the sand had stopped.

"What is it?" Derick asked.

After a moment's pause, I pulled my hand away. "Hmmm, nothing. I had thought I saw something before. I guess I had imagined it."

The two of us finally left the tree for the warmer SUV that sat in the middle of main street where I had left it. As I drove, I held Derick's hand in mine in silence. I had intended to go back to the gala but when I saw the barn and all the people, I just kept driving. I wanted to see my children. I wanted them to feel the peace we had found and to know the comfort of us being a family again.

Part of me didn't care what happened with the gala, and the other part knew I had planned it so well that I didn't actually need to be there to see it succeed. My success would be with me regardless of how well I did as a party planner or designer. I knew that now and didn't need to seek out praise or confirmation for my worth from sources outside myself. I was enough and so was Derick and together, we could be perfect for each other.

As I drove, I thought back on the hourglass ornament and on the peace I had craved so badly only a few nights ago. I'd decided the magic that I thought I'd seen in the hourglass could be a part of me. I could slow down and take the time I needed when it was necessary. I could be happy and content without the opinion or praise of others and I could do it with Derick by my side.

Derick

The five of us snuggled around the haphazardly decorated Christmas tree that night and ate the chocolates I had intended for Ivy. I slept in my home that night, with my children and my wife under the same roof. It had never felt so good to be home and I promised to always remember the blessing it was to have a place where I felt needed. Christmas morning was anything but quiet and I relished in the noise that came with my family. I had no problem leaving my studio apartment behind for good, and was half tempted to not even clean the place out. Had it not been an inconvenience to Al, I might have left it all to avoid the pain of walking through those doors again.

Later that Christmas afternoon, Ivy drove me to check on my truck. I'd already called Oliver to meet me with a tow, but wanted to get some of my personal things out first. As I approached that old beat up thing, I decided I wanted to crawl in it one last time. I pulled the Christmas gift I'd gotten for Ivy off the passenger seat and held it in my lap while, out of habit, I pulled the keys from my pocket and stuck them in the ignition. I gave the steering wheel a fist bump and then turned the key.

To my astonishment, the darn thing started right up. I couldn't believe it. Ivy whooped and hollered from outside the truck. It hadn't given up on me after all.

Ives slid into the passenger seat and smiled up at me.

"Want to go for a ride?" she asked.

I held out the present I'd gotten her in response. She looked at me in shock. "I thought you'd taken my gift back."

"I did. This is a new one. A homemade version."

She pulled the wrapping paper back as the engine of my truck roared and I pulled out onto the street. Her laughter was the purest and most free sound I'd heard from her ever before and I knew I'd be happy if it was the only sound I ever heard again.

The End

NEXT IN THE HOLLY SPRINGS SERIES

Re-Gifting Christmas

Jane was sure she'd find her dream PR job and didn't expect her marriage to be over before its first Christmas, but she was wrong on both accounts. Being divorced and jobless Jane returns home to Holly Springs, the last place she wants her failures to be publicized. Soon everyone in the small town knows about her, but it isn't until she reconnects with Oliver, her high school sweetheart that someone finally knows her.

Oliver was sure he'd buried his feelings for Jane and that nothing could upend his comfortable life but he was wrong on both accounts. Taking over his family's salvage yard and finding a talent for turning trash into treasure, the last thing he wants are reminders of past heartbreak. Crossing paths with Jane scratches at the surface of the pain he worked hard to bury. He attempts to avoid all things Jane until he learns of her recent divorce.

Will Jane be able to pick up the shattered pieces of her self-worth and will Oliver finally put Jane ahead of his fear?

If so, will they be able to re-gift their hearts to each other in time for Christmas?

ABOUT THE AUTHOR

Matt and Tiffini are the best friend, crazy in love duo behind M.T. Knights. The couple met while working together at a catering office in Salt Lake City, Utah. Tiffini knew within minutes of meeting Matt that if he ever asked her to marry him, she would say yes. It didn't take long for Matt to come to the same conclusion and their friendship quickly turned into their very own happily ever after. From the floor of their tiny one-bedroom apartment as newlyweds where they read novels together, to creating their first manuscript as a couple, they found that emotions are often best told and felt in the written language.

Since then, the two have spent many, otherwise empty nights creating stories and worlds with each other and turning them into novels. When they are not writing or editing, they enjoy spending time with their four kids, giant dog and persnickety cat. They can be found on soccer fields or basketball courts cheering their kids on, hiking in the mountains of Utah or fishing with their crew in the many lakes or ponds surrounding their home.

Made in the USA
Middletown, DE
16 December 2023